# Reasons

# Reasons

 A Tale of Romance

DAVID SCOTT

Copyright © David Scott.

All rights reserved. No part of this book may be reproduced in any form or by any electronic or mechanical means, including information storage and retrieval systems, without permission in writing from the publisher, except by reviewers, who may quote brief passages in a review.

ISBN:  978-1-64970-024-7   (Paperback Edition)
ISBN:  978-1-64970-025-4   (Hardcover Edition)
ISBN:  978-1-64970-022-3   (E-book Edition)

Some characters and events in this book are fictitious. Any similarity to real persons, living or dead, is coincidental and not intended by the author.

**Book Ordering Information**

Phone Number: 347-901-4929 or 347-901-4920
Email: info@globalsummithouse.com
Global Summit House
www.globalsummithouse.com

Printed in the United States of America

# Contents

Chapter 1: Laguna Beach Rendezvous .................................................. 1
Chapter 2: Breakfast ........................................................................ 14
Chapter 3: Lunch ............................................................................ 28
Chapter 4: Dinner ........................................................................... 84
Chapter 5: Closing Time .................................................................. 99
Chapter 6: C'est Si Bon .................................................................. 133
Chapter 7: Reasons ........................................................................ 148

# Chapter 1

## Laguna Beach Rendezvous

**Vic Fontaine**

April 19, 2019 is a beautiful day as I am driving northbound on the South Pacific Coast Highway from my home in Laguna Niguel heading for the beach town of Laguna Beach, California.

I hope the sunscreen I generously applied to my face doesn't start running into my eyes. Ever since I had skin cancer surgery on my nose a few years ago I've made sure I go outside with sunscreen on my face, especially when I will be outside on a sunny day for at least an hour. If things go well today longer than that.

My classic 1967 red Camaro is purring like a kitten. It's my most prized possession. It costs me a small fortune to maintain and insure. It is worth every penny.

This drive was years in the making.

I am reviewing the sequence of events that are leading to my Laguna Beach rendezvous with Dulce Bravo.

I've been waiting twelve years since 2007 wondering what if. I haven't seen Dulce in twelve years.

When did my attraction to Dulce first begin? In the mail room? What stands out are the mail room and the hallway and the perfume caper. It began in the mail room at Johnson Industrial Supply in Commerce, California fourteen years ago when I joined the company in mid-2005 for the first time.

Disoriented and mentally beat up after a long bout of unemployment and caring for my sick wife Lynn being hired at Johnson was a blessing.

Several days after being hired I was in the mail room checking my mail slot for mail when somebody walking up from behind asked me a question.

"Were you in the Hitler Youth?"

I turned and looked to my left and saw a woman removing mail from her mail slot. It not so much that she was attractive. She was attractive. But something else was at work transcending her looks, which were very good to be sure.

I detected a Mona Lisa smile on her face as she precipitously walked away leaving me astonished.

Dulce Bravo was the name on the placard underneath her mail slot.

At that moment in the mail room I fell for her. I've been falling for her ever since.

---

I feel happy anticipation building up within me. I have a smile on my face.

I was the Accounting Supervisor and Dulce worked in Order Entry. I saw her several times during those first weeks of my new employment.

When I was taken around being introduced to my new coworkers Dulce wasn't present.

A month after Dulce asked me that odd question in the mail room another milestone was reached.

I remember that day clearly. It was almost quitting time. I had just returned to my office from a meeting with the owner.

My office door was open. I looked up and saw Dulce standing about fifteen feet from my office. She was having a conversation with a coworker. I could just barely make out what they were saying.

Earlier in the day I detected a cold sore beginning to form on my lower lip. I felt compelled to share this information with Dulce.

I put down the notes from a meeting with my boss that I was going to transcribe and urgently searched for Dulce's company email address.

I began composing an email to Dulce as she and the other person walked away.

Because she was leaving for the day, Dulce wouldn't read my email until tomorrow. I knew at the time she would consider it off the wall, but I couldn't help myself. It was an impulsive spur of the moment act. I was compelled by forces I couldn't control.

> *Hi Dulce,*
>
> *I am beginning to have a cold sore. I am going to gargle with salt water tonight.*
>
> *Vic*

Driving home I recall being puzzled why I would send Dulce that email. My email to her was almost as odd as her question to me in the mail room. Then after being home for an hour it occurred to me.

I liked Dulce and I didn't know why.

I like Dulce now and I still don't know why.

If I am honest with myself, I love Dulce. I told her that I love her in some of my emails conveyed to her via our mutual acquaintance Marisol.

Do I love her? I mean for real?

What is love? Does anyone really know? Is that why most songs are about love?

---

I am crossing into Laguna Beach. My rendezvous with Dulce in Laguna Beach at the gazebo is scheduled for ten this morning. I feel a glow in my heart.

I am turning right onto Broadway Street. With luck I will find a parking spot.

There's one!

I'm easing into my spot. I'm always excited when I find a parking spot.

I'm pumping the meter full of quarters.

It is nine-fifty.

After adjusting my hat for maximum protection against the sun I begin walking to the gazebo rendezvous point.

I cross Pacific Coast Highway, also known as PCH, and pivot right with the beach and basketball court on my left. Smell that ocean.

I'm climbing up the steep flight of stairs leading up to the path and the gazebo. I begin my ascent hoping I am not on a fool's errand.

It would hurt beyond words to be stood up. It would be devastating to my self-esteem and so much more. I could be setting myself up for heartbreak.

Just as I am two stairs away from the top, I feel a twinge in my lower back. I stop and access the situation. I can still walk, but there is a localized discomfort. Why does something like this have to happen on this day of all days?

---

## Dulce Bravo

I'm riding shotgun in my brother Joaquin's car. We are driving along PCH. I am wondering why I agreed to this meeting with Vic Fontaine whom I haven't seen since 2007. That's twelve years ago.

At the time Fontaine didn't seem to mean anything to me. Well, maybe that isn't totally accurate. What about now? I suppose that is why I agreed to meet him.

What really surprised me were the emails and Valentine's Day card Fontaine sent me care of my friend Marisol who still works at Johnson Industrial Supply where Fontaine and I once worked. What would cause him to send such emails and a Valentine's Day card professing his love for me after such a long time? Has he been pining for me for twelve years?

In my view that email brought into question Fontaine's mental health status. That is also the view of my brothers Joaquin and Gustavo.

His last email inviting me to this meeting intrigued me enough that in spite of my better judgement it tipped the balance in favor of my decision to meet with him.

We are in stop and go traffic in Huntington Beach. It is 9:20 am.

I am happy it is a beautiful day. A perfect Chamber of Commerce day.

I remember the email reply I gave Fontaine through Marisol:

*Fontaine,*

*I agree to meet you on the date and time and place you indicated in Laguna Beach.*

*Bravo*

I always called him by his last name Fontaine.

I remember the first time I noticed Fontaine. It was in the mail room fourteen years ago.

It's not like he was good looking. Cute maybe. He was kind of good looking in a nerdy way. He was and is ten years older than me. For some reason I remember that factoid. I am now 43 years old and that would make him 53 years old now. Making matters worse at the time he was a married man.

Fontaine said he's a widower in one of his emails. I didn't tell him my marital status. Does he know I am divorced and single? Marisol told me she never actually spoke to Fontaine. It was all done by email and text.

Marisol also claimed I know everything she knows since she shared all of his emails and texts with me and her replies. No mention was made that I am now single. There is Jorge who likes me and he is a nice guy, but he is not boyfriend material. I am not saying Fontaine is mind you.

There was something about him that intrigued me. What was it? I didn't have a clue then and I haven't got a clue now. That's untrue. I do know.

Whatever my feelings for Fontaine are, indifference is not one of them. I am not indifferent to Fontaine. I think this is why I agreed to meet with him. Not think, I know this is why I agreed to meet with him to answer the question of why I am not indifferent to him.

I recollect saying something admittedly peculiar to him in the mail room, but I can't remember exactly what it was despite what he claims in his email.

He claims in one of his emails I asked him if he had been in the Hitler Youth.

Did I ask him that question?

I think I did.

Was I nervous when I said that, or if I said that?

'The Sound of Music'. He mentioned that movie in one of his emails.

I had watched 'The Sound of Music' the night before.

What about that weird email Fontaine sent me something about his having a cold sore?

At the time I thought it was strange for him to do that. I still do.

Was he flirting with me? Oh yeah, he was flirting with me in an offbeat kind of way.

The biggest elephant in the room is the public trial last year that lasted two months in which Fontaine was acquitted of laundering drug money through a now bankrupt company called Genome Genetics.

I remember the headline in the Los Angeles Times.

### Vic Fontaine Acquitted of Laundering Drug Money in Genome Genetics Scandal
### Trial Lasted Two Months and Cost L.A. County Taxpayers $1.3 Million Dollars

I bite my lip as I feel my breathing increasing slightly thinking about meeting up with a guy I last knew and last saw in 2007 who only last year had been accused of being a big-time major player drug dealer. I try to ignore the obvious. The possibility this might be true excites me.

"Are you awake?" Joaquin asks me shaking my shoulder as I was dozing off. Why am I smiling?

"We're in Laguna Beach. I don't understand why you are agreeing to meet this guy. I'll ask you one more time. What if he is a nut job? What if he is still involved with dealing drugs?" Joaquin is asking me these questions with genuine concern in his voice.

"Then I'll text you and you'll come pick me up. You said you were going to hang around Laguna today anyway since you don't get down here that often. Don't forget he was found not guilty of laundering drug money."

"How did he get involved with the Cartel to begin with? That is what I want to know. I saw the emails Vic Fontaine sent you. Looks like a nut job to me. He could be a stalker. Gustavo agrees with me. Why are you meeting him at a gazebo? I should tag along with you. He doesn't know who I am. He might not remember what you look like."

"Fontaine might have problems, but he is harmless," I reply hoping that is true. "He might be a no show. If that is the case, we can have brunch at that nice restaurant overlooking the ocean I told you about. Drop me off, park downtown and do your thing. I'll be fine."

"This Fontaine guy isn't dealing with a full deck," my brother skeptically replies. "I still don't understand why you didn't drive your own car."

"So that you can protect me like a big brother should," I say as convincingly as I can.

"Then I'll come with you."

"No!" I respond adamantly. I am surprised how insistent I am that Joaquin not go with me to the gazebo. "Just wait around for me like we've discussed."

I see the basketball court on the right as we drive by. According to the Google map the walkway up to the gazebo is nearby.

"Pull over," I'm telling Joaquin as he eases the car over.

"One last chance to change your mind," Joaquin says insistently.

"Have fun," I tell my big brother as I exit his car. "I'll keep you updated by text."

"Don't give Fontaine your phone number or email or home or work address," Joaquin cautions me as a last piece of brotherly advice.

I check the time. It is ten o'clock.

Why did I agree to meet Fontaine?

Why didn't I drive my own car?

Why do I want to meet Fontaine alone?

Why do I really want to meet Fontaine in the first place?

My mind keeps returning to his drug money laundering trial.

But there is much more to it than his trial.

I have an empty place in my heart that yearns to be filled.

## Vic Fontaine

It's exactly ten o'clock. I'm at our agreed to rendezvous time and place and the gazebo is empty. I can see Santa Catalina Island. The oldies song '26 Miles (Santa Catalina)' comes to mind. I love listening to oldies. I gaze at the ocean remembering how this all came about.

Dreams about Dulce began intruding on my sleep about six months ago. Then came the bouts of crying. What would be the reason for that? I haven't seen Dulce for twelve years. That alone would be a big giveaway my thoughts are irrational. I am ready to accept that conclusion.

Being a widower might have had something to do with it. I lost my dear wife Lynn to pneumonia after she'd suffered off and on from bronchitis most of her life. Lynn's battle with diabetes didn't help and her bipolar condition almost guaranteed her a premature death.

I never physically cheated on Lynn with Dulce. It was emotional cheating not physical, which from my perspective was worse.

I pursued urgent attempts to find Dulce. I was able to contact Marisol a mutual acquaintance of ours from our time together at Johnson Industrial Supply. Luckily for me Marisol agreed to be the go between for Dulce and me. Through Marisol I was able to send Dulce several email messages.

Dulce agreed to meet me and today's the day.

My therapist told me I was suffering morbid grief due to Lynn's death and experiencing Post-Traumatic Stress Disorder, or PTSD.

She told me in her opinion I was also exhibiting symptoms of hypomania, but she couldn't definitively give me a firm diagnosis without more sessions. I think she said only a medical doctor could make that determination. Not sure.

Even though I am a layperson I know from online research and my own past I am hypomanic, which I also know has helped my career at times. At times I guess it has also been a detriment as well depending on the circumstances.

I am going over in my mind of one email that was forwarded to Dulce by Marisol requesting our rendezvous. My therapist said it was particularly revealing. My therapist didn't know that email was far less lovey-dovey than others I sent to Dulce via Marisol.

My therapist concluded my feelings for Dulce are real albeit in an obsessive way. She recommended it would be wise for me to be cautious meeting Dulce after all this time especially if her marital status is in question.

Although I don't know if Dulce is married or not, or if she has a boyfriend or not, by agreeing to meet me this must not be an issue for her. My notoriety from the drug money laundering trial must not be an issue for her either.

Remembering the highlights of the email makes me uncomfortable and embarrassed and happy at the same time. I omitted any reference to my public trial.

*Marisol please forward this to Dulce :) :) :)*

*Hi Dulce,*

*Vic Fontaine here. I hope all is well with you and your family.*

*I understand if you were surprised by my recent communications. What's up with this guy who was a married man who put perfume named after me in my mailbox at work? And then 12 years later out of the blue suddenly wants to chat with me?*

*It's admittedly complicated and I would like very much to explain the series of events that occurred that lead up to the perfume incident and my subsequent recent behavior.*

*I get it if you are married and have a life and I don't want to upset that apple cart. I want you to be happy in every way.*

*All I would like is the opportunity to explain it to you.*

*If you would please meet on Friday April 19, 2019 in Laguna Beach at the gazebo on the bluffs at 10:00 am I can explain everything to you.*

*If you don't respond to this message, I will accept it as a yes to our meeting.*

*I took the liberty of providing you with my phone number at the bottom and you have my email address already, but I listed it too.*

*See you then!*

*Vic*

## Dulce Bravo

The contents of Fontaine's many emails are battering my brain as I begin my climb up the stairs toward the gazebo.

I reach the summit.

There it is! There's the gazebo. I am self-conscious thinking I should have touched up the grey streak in my hair. I have gained weight. I know I look good in my dress and heels.

Did I dress up for Fontaine?

I gather my wits and with some happy trepidation I begin walking to it.

Why happy trepidation? Isn't trepidation a bad thing?

## Vic Fontaine

It is ten minutes after ten. My message specified ten. Lots could have happened. Traffic. An emergency. Car problems. I gave Dulce my email address and phone number. She can call or text me.

The ocean breeze feels and smells good.

A welcome voice interrupts my silence.

"Fontaine?"

I turn around. It is Dulce. She looks great and is wearing a flattering dress. I hope the passage of time, twelve years to be exact, has been as good to me as it has been to her. I have gained weight. I've also developed a receding hairline camouflaged by my hat.

She slowly enters the gazebo as I put the back of my palms on the railing looking at her.

"Thank you for coming," I say noticing a streak of grey in her long thick luxurious black hair that has an appeal to it.

She says nothing and walks up to the railing as two adults and a small child wander into the gazebo.

I turn around standing next to her. We're looking down at the rocks and ocean.

## Dulce Bravo

Fontaine isn't what you would call a hunk, but he does look great in that tailored sports coat despite having put on some weight. He looks cute in that hat. What did I just think? No way.

"It's a nice day," I say staring straight ahead relishing the look on Vic's face when he first saw me.

"It is a nice day," Vic replies after a prolonged pause.

The three people depart the gazebo.

We are alone again.

# Chapter 2

## *Breakfast*

"Would you like to get some breakfast?" Vic nervously asks realizing his hands are tremoring and his heart is skipping a beat. What's with this?

"Sure," Dulce replies feeling a rapid flutter in her chest and a happy anticipation. Say what?

Vic gestures for Dulce to exit the gazebo first making him feel gallant.

Dulce is doing her best to discern if Vic is a nut job like Joaquin believes he is.

They walk off the path stepping over some plants and shrubs and into the open-air patio dining area of a restaurant overlooking the ocean.

A greeter awaits them. Not knowing if a reservation is required Vic covertly hands the greeter a twenty-dollar bill and whispers for a table in a private location on the patio. Vic and Dulce are shown to a corner table.

A waiter strolls over with a menu. Vic discreetly gives the waiter two twenty-dollar bills to gain the waiter's loyalty. Somebody said all is fair in love and war.

"May I start you off with coffee, orange juice?"

Dulce and Vic are flapping their unopened menus around like fans.

"Coffee will be fine," Dulce manages to say.
"Make it two," Vic follows.

The waiter departs leaving Dulce and Vic alone again.

They both begin to fake immerse themselves in their menus.

"I ah, I think I'll have the Eggs Benedict," Vic mutters, not caring what he orders.

"Eggs Benedict works for me," Dulce states.

Vic's never had Eggs Benedict before.

"I understand the Eggs Benedict here are delicious," Vic says to Dulce using an innocent lie to launch into an attempt at small talk.

The waiter returns in the nick of time to temporarily dispel any awkwardness.

"Orders of Eggs Benedict for both of us," Vic says as confidently as he can. "Orange juice too and coffee refills."

"Would you like your Eggs Benedict to be Royale?"

"Of course," Vic quickly replies, having no idea what the waiter means.

"Very good. Two Eggs Royale coming up." The waiter gathers their menus.

Vic glances at Dulce, who reciprocates.

"It's a nice day," she says under her breath.

"Pardon?" he asks.

"It's a nice day."

"It is. It's a nice day. I believe we both agree it is a nice day. And it is one heck of a nice day."

They both blurt out, "I was-"

They smile again.

"You go first," Vic manages to say to Dulce almost inaudibly.

"The emails you sent me. They had some very interesting things in them."

Vic feels a defensive wall forming around his psyche.

"About that. You need to know a few things. I was in an unusually candid frame of mind."

"I'll say you were," Dulce retorts, then backs off. So far Fontaine doesn't seem like a nut case.

Vic takes a deep breath. Might as well not postpone the inevitable.

"Why did you ask me if I was in the Hitler Youth?"
"I didn't."
"Yes, you did. Why would I make that up? You can't make that up."

Vic feels himself getting a little angry at her denial briefly overriding any feelings of embarrassment talking to Dulce about his emails.

Dulce furrows her brow as the waiter brings orange juice and refills their coffee cups.

They take long sips of coffee. Dulce confesses to herself she did ask Fontaine that question. Why not just admit it?
"Okay Fontaine, you got me. I did ask that question."

"Why? It was a strange question to ask me."

Dulce sighs knowing this is the weak link in her chain. Might as well take it head on.

"Why did I ask you that question? It's complicated. It was strange. Okay? I admit that."

Vic harkens back to a pleasant memory and shares it with Dulce whether she wants to hear it or not.

"That night, after you asked me that question, I was on a natural high. I couldn't stop thinking about you. I kept thinking to myself, 'Who says that'?"

"What about your emails and The Valentine's Day card?" she asks changing the subject.

"I'm willing to talk about my emails and the VD card."

"Very good. We'll talk about that next."

The waiter arrives with their Eggs Royale.

"Is this fish?" Dulce asks the waiter.

"Smoked salmon."

"I'm allergic to salmon. I'm also allergic to cod and tuna. I avoid fish altogether."

Vic shakes his head in disbelief. Did somebody say Murphy's Law?

He tries to salvage the situation.

"Bring us pancakes and lots of butter and syrup," Vic tells the waiter.

"You're not allergic to pancakes, are you?" Vic asks Dulce.

"No. Except they aren't good for the waistline."

"Let's live dangerously," Vic says, beginning to feel more relaxed.

"Trust me your waistline looks fine," he says boldly.

Vic reaches over and grabs Dulce's Eggs Royale.

"Waste not, want not," he opines.

The waiter departs.

"You were saying?" Vic asks.

Dulce chuckles despite herself.

"You looked, that is, at that moment I asked you if you'd been in the Hitler Youth you looked so blond."

"Blond?" Vic asks, realizing he still has his hat on. He needs to apply more sunscreen. Vic removes his hat displaying substantially less blond hair than he had twelve years ago.

"As you can see, I'm not as blond as I used to be. What did you mean by I looked so blond?"

He removes the small tube of sunscreen from his sports jacket pocket and begins applying it.

Vic doesn't give Dulce a chance to answer his question and veers off topic.

"I had skin cancer surgery a few years ago on my nose. I had what is called Squamous a somewhat dangerous type of melanoma if left untreated. I had surgery on my nose."

Vic points to the tip of his nose.

"See that indention? They had to go in and take the cancer out. It was an outpatient surgery."

"I'm glad you were able to catch it in time."

"Me too. It was my coworkers who encouraged me to check it out after this red bump on my nose wouldn't go away."

Dulce realizes she is thankful Fontaine doesn't have skin cancer. Naturally. She wouldn't wish that on anybody, right? Could it be more than that? She only knows she's relieved he doesn't have skin cancer.

He finishes applying the second coat of sunscreen on his head and face and especially his nose and returns the hat to the top of his head.

"You were telling me how blond I looked in the mail room."

"Yes. You see, you were the only the second or third Caucasian other than the owners who worked at Johnson in a mostly Hispanic work force. You stood out."

"You mean I was a conspicuous white boy who stood out with blond hair and all."

"That is one way to put it," Dulce says sheepishly.

"What's that got to do with asking me if I was in the Hitler Youth? First of all, it was a youth organization in Nazi Germany in the 1930s. You know I couldn't have possibly been in that organization. If I had been, I would be well into my nineties by now maybe over a hundred. Second of all I am an American and I don't have German ancestry. I'm of Irish, Scottish and English ancestry as far as I know."

Vic believes he has the initiative. He is going to push the envelope.

"The Hitler Youth question you asked me has to do with the movie doesn't it?"

"What movie?" Dulce asks cautiously her shields up.

"'The Sound of Music'."

Dulce looks away. He said that one of his infamous emails to Marisol. How does he know this? She knows that is a big reason why she is sitting in a restaurant patio with Fontaine having breakfast overlooking the Pacific Ocean in Laguna Beach. The fact he somehow knew about 'The Sound of Music'. That and his drug money laundering trial. And other things too.

"Fontaine you got me. It had to do with 'The Sound of Music'."

Vic is beaming saying to himself, "I knew it I knew it."

"Let me guess. For some reason I reminded you of the character Rolf in the movie who goes from being a telegram delivery boy to a Nazi and joins the Hitler Youth."

Vic pauses, gazing at Dulce now without any apprehension. He decides he needs to educate Dulce on one of the nuances of the movie.

"Except Rolf didn't join the Hitler Youth," Vic pontificates as he begins to mansplain. "He actually joined what was called the SA or storm troopers. They were also called brownshirts. I know this from the uniform he was wearing."

It was obvious to Dulce that Fontaine had watched the movie and researched this. Hitler Youth, SA, whatever.

The waiter arrives with the pancakes. Good timing Dulce thinks.

I'll bring you refills on your coffee," the waiter says.

Dulce and Vic are eating their food with ardor because they are hungry.

Vic swallows and begins talking.

"These pancakes are delicious. Back to the mail room. I'm thinking you were linking me to Rolf in 'The Sound of Music' because I am blond and he was blond. I know you want to know how I was able to guess that."

Vic then says, "Thinking you were linking. That rhymes."

Dulce grins despite her best efforts not to grin.

"I do want to know. It's a reason I agreed to meet you. Curiosity. How did you know my liking that movie relates to what I said to you that day about the Hitler Youth?"

"Intuition. Have you heard of Dr. Eric Berne? He made ground breaking studies about intuition. Check it out for yourself google Eric Berne and intuition. When I came on board at Johnson, I had experienced a tough eleven months of unemployment and almost became homeless. My wife Lynn was in and out of hospitals with various health problems."

As Dulce was about to google the keywords Eric Berne and intuition her iPhone pings with a text message.

"Excuse me," Dulce said as she checks the text. It's from Joaquin.

*"Are you alright? Where are you? I am at the gazebo now. Tell me where you are."*

Dulce feels herself getting irritated at Joaquin and texts him back.

*"I'm fine Joaquin. Please don't worry. Go play a pickup game of basketball. Take a walk along the beach. I am with Fontaine and we are talking. Thank you for your concern. I will keep you updated."*

While Dulce is texting her brother, Vic is wolfing down Eggs Royale and pancakes.

"It was my brother Joaquin wanting to know how I am."
"What did you tell him?" Vic asks between chews.
"I told him I am fine. Go on. Tell me about your intuition."

Vic puts down his fork and wipes his mouth.

"How would a Hispanic person like yourself even know anything about the Hitler Youth? I'm just saying it is an obscure thing for someone with your background, or for someone with any background for that matter, to know about much less ask a question about. It was logical to assume that question had a prompt. I just had a gut feeling that prompt was 'The Sound of Music'. Simple as that."

"Simple as that?" Dulce asks, starting to feel comfortable discussing this topic with Fontaine.

"Simple as that. I used my intuition. Look it, there's something you need to know. When I started working at Johnson my intuition was at a fever pitch. If you do some research on intuition and Eric Berne you'll find out. I was suffering from massive sleep deficits and that was a reason why as I was so intuitive especially regarding you. Intuition works better when you haven't had enough sleep."

Dulce feels there is more for Fontaine to share with her.

"Let's assume you are correct and I did associate you with Rolf in 'The Sound of Music'."

"Assume?" Vic interjects.

"Allow me to say that again. You are correct no assumptions. But why do you think I said that to you? I don't know myself for sure."

Dulce knows that comment is only half true. She has her own theory and wants to hear Fontaine's.

"You said, 'I don't know myself for sure', which tells me you have some idea," Vic said, staring at Dulce. "I'll tell you why. You projected feelings onto me the female character in 'The Sound of Music' had for Rolf. I was Rolf at that instant in the mail room and you were what's her face Liesl I think her name was. That was her name. Liesl."

Vic unleashed his sledgehammer.

"You like me, don't you?"

Dulce looks at Vic.

"That remains to be seen."

"Really?" Vic replies, disappointed. Then again, she can't admit she likes me, he thinks.

"I know you like me," Dulce counters.

"That remains to be seen," Vic says with a hint of embarrassment in his voice because he has already told Dulce half a dozen times over the course of half a dozen emails and in a Valentine's Day card delivered by his surrogate Marisol that he loves her. Not likes her. Loves her.

They have reached an early impasse.

Vic begins eating Dulce's Eggs Royale. Dulce delves into her pancakes as the attentive waiter approaches.

"Will this be on one check or on separate checks?"

Vic smiles and says nothing. To his surprise Dulce speaks up.

"I'll take it," she says to the waiter.

The waiter dutifully makes out the check and hands it to Dulce as Vic continues munching.

"I'll pick up lunch," Vic finally says.

"I won't be here for lunch or dinner Fontaine," Dulce caustically states.

"Are you mad at me?" Vic inquires.

"No. I have to leave soon that's all."

"But we're just getting acquainted," Vic replies, seeing his grand plan crumbling before his eyes.

"Why do you call me Fontaine? My name is Vic. Not Fontaine. Vic."

"Fontaine is your last name."

Vic realizes he is beginning to feel agitated.

"You know darn well what I mean. I would appreciate it if you would call me Vic."

Dulce rolls her eyes.

"Okay, VIC!"

"I'm glad we got that straightened out. I guess you'll be moving along now. Thanks for breakfast. Or brunch whatever this is we are eating."

Dulce laughs.

"You're not going to dodge giving me an explanation about those emails and Valentines' Day card you sent to me by Marisol. Did you ever think it might embarrass me you sending all of those emails to Marisol? I have a feeling Marisol shared everything you sent me through her with a lot of people we both know. It was probably discussed on social media. You and me were big time juicy gossip fodder Fontaine."

"If I had known your email address, I would have sent the emails and VD card directly to you. Nobody would tell me. It was my impression you and Marisol are best buds."

"Your impression was way off the mark. We're casual friends that's all."

Vic was becoming disheartened.

"Your email address was highly classified and I didn't have the necessary security clearance."

Vic pauses.

"You're not leaving?" he asks.

"Not until I get some answers and an explanation."

"About what?"

"About your emails and card."

"You already said you know I like you. Is that a felony?"

"It might be in some jurisdictions."

Dulce's phone pings once more. It's Joaquin.

*"When are you leaving? I've already walked up and down several streets downtown and I'm ready to leave. Where are you?"*

Vic is scrutinizing Dulce's expression.

"Is that Joaquin again?"

"Maybe."

"Why does he keep texting you?"

"He is concerned you're a nut case."

"What did you tell him?"

"I told him I'm not sure yet."

"I'm in complete control of my faculties," Vic says.

Dulce texts Joaquin.

*"Go home. I'm going to be here for a while longer."*

Joaquin immediately replies.

*"Are you sure? Has Fontaine tried to put the moves on you yet?"*

*"No. I'll take a cab home. Don't worry about me. Bye."*

Dulce resumes eating her pancakes.

Vic resumes eating Dulce's Eggs Royale.

It's getting close to one o'clock in the afternoon. They have stretched out their food having talked much more than they have eaten.

The waiter who waited on them this morning managed to get the afternoon waiter to let him take his shift. He knows a budding romance when he sees one and he wants to see it play out. Soon the entire staff knows. It is always entertaining to watch them.

Besides, the guy is a good tipper to a fault.

"Why did you email me about your cold sore?" Dulce says as the restaurant staff begins to give Dulce and Vic looks and pointing at them.
"I thought it was something you needed to know."
"That is what is called Too Much Information Fontaine. TMI."

They finally manage to finish all of the food on their plates.

Dulce and Vic continue to give each other furtive glances. Vic breaks the deadlock.

"Why did you turn me into Lucia the HR Manager?"
"Surely you jest," Dulce responds.
"Surely, I do not. Do you know how traumatizing that was for me?"
"For you? Give me a break. What about me? Putting a bottle of Dulce Bravo perfume in my mail slot. I mean really. Weren't you married at the time? Why did you do such a thing?"

"That bottle costs me almost one hundred dollars and that was twelve years ago no thirteen years ago it was in 2006. I don't think they make Dulce Bravo perfume any more. Did you notice it had your name on the bottle?"

"I noticed. Weren't you married at the time?"

"Lynn found that bottle two years later and I had to lie to her that it was an anniversary gift I was going to give her. If you had accepted the perfume I wouldn't have had to lie to Lynn."

Dulce laughs at Vic's convoluted logic noticing he declined to answer her question about his being married at the time. She thinks he must be saying this with his tongue in his cheek.

"I have exculpatory evidence," Vic utters in a whiny tone.
"Exculpatory what?"
"You don't know what that is," Vic states in a mocking tone.
"I know this Fontaine. Whatever exculpatory evidence is you don't have it. In my legal opinion you don't have plausible deniability."

Vic takes a sip of coffee thinking Dulce looks cute. Plausible deniability. Why does she have to be so cute?

"Did you know Lucia told me I was guilty of sexual harassment? I told her it wasn't sexual harassment because it had your name on the bottle. I had to take a refresher sexual harassment training course. I could have gone to Lucia and complained about the Hitler Youth question. You only asked me that question because I'm white because the guys in the Hitler Youth were white."

"Are you playing the race card now?" Dulce says not really meaning it. "You know that's not why I asked you that question. What about you? Going to Lucia telling her I was creating a hostile work environment. I don't believe I was creating a hostile work environment. It was a trumped-up accusation because you were mad at me. Do you know how traumatizing that was for me?"

Vic swells up with feelings of genuine regret and then apologizes.

"I wish I hadn't done that. I'm so sorry for the trauma I caused you."

He means it and is revisiting the guilt he felt remembering how Lucia had told him that Dulce had cried when she was told about his hostile work environment complaint.

Vic tries to muzzle his emotions and looks down at the ground.

"The last thing in the world I wanted to do was hurt you," he says his voice cracking with guilt.

Vic isn't sure, but Dulce seems to be smiling enigmatically. There seems to be a light in her eyes.

If Vic didn't know better, he would swear that Dulce is glowing. Is she being inscrutable?

Vic does not know what Dulce is thinking and what she wants.

Dulce knows what Vic is thinking and what he wants.

# Chapter 3

## *Lunch*

"Are you going to be ordering lunch?" their waiter asks appearing out of nowhere.

"We are," Vic says smiling at Dulce. "If you would bring us some menus."

The waiter gives them two menus he is holding.

"What if I am ready to leave?" Dulce asks.
"My intuition says you are not."
"You and your friend Eric Berne huh Vic?"
"My friend Eric and me."

"What would you like Bravo, I mean Dulce?"
"If you will allow me time to study the menu, I will let you know."
"Get what you want. It's on me."
"Glad you told me. Now I can look at the expensive side of the menu."

"May I get you anything to drink?" the waiter asks.
"Yes," Vic replies. "I'd like a greyhound."

The waiter turns his attention to Dulce.

"And for you?"
"A glass of red wine. For the anti-oxidants."

They study the lunch menu.

The waiter returns with their drinks and water. Vic eagerly takes a long swig. Dulce takes a small sip.

"I am going to have a Caesar's Salad and steak and lobster enchiladas," she says.

"What a coincidence," Vic mentions. "I was going to order the exact same thing. I hope you don't mind."

"Not at all."

The waiter returns and takes their orders.

Vic finishes his greyhound and asks the waiter to bring him a rum and coke.

Dulce sees the alcohol is loosening Vic's tongue.
"Your brother is right. I am nuts about you."
"He thinks you are a nut job. You shouldn't mix drinks."
"What?"
"You ordered a greyhound, which is gin or vodka with grapefruit juice. Now you are ordering a rum and coke. You shouldn't drink vodka and rum at the same time."
"Are you a bartender in another life?"
"No. I'm just telling you something everybody knows."
"I'm everybody and I didn't know. Back to your brother."
"What about him?"
"He's right. I am nuts about you."
"Maybe you should drop the 'about you' part."

The waiter returns with Vic's rum and coke.
"To an interesting afternoon," he toasts downing his drink in one long gulp.

"Ours is a complicated situation," Vic says to Dulce. "It has a lot of moving parts."
"Moving parts? You make it sound like a production line."

Vic suddenly realizes something.

"I've got to go pump quarters in the meter or I'll get a parking ticket."
"You still drive that red classic Camaro?"
"You remember my car?"
"It was the only classic red Camaro in the employee parking lot."

He slowly stands up and visibly winces due to the pulled muscle in his lower back he acquired while climbing up the stairs to the gazebo rendezvous point.

"Can you walk?" Dulce asks half seriously.
"Yes, I've been walking since I was a small child. I shall return."
"That's what I was afraid of."

Vic tries to cover the growing anxiety building up in him.

"Don't go away," he begs. "If you do bounce here is money to cover my tab." Vic removes two twenty-dollar bills from his wallet and puts them on the table in front of Dulce.

"Please don't leave me. I won't be long."
"Thanks for the warning."

Vic walks away unsteadily going into the restaurant exiting through the back-entrance walking through the parking lot toward PCH. Vic almost bumps into a lady walking her dog as he rounds the corner to the sidewalk. His desperation is camouflaging the pain in his lower back.

He is in panic mode now. The song 'Got to Get You into My Life' by the band 'Earth Wind and Fire' starts playing in his mind. He had heard it on the oldies station the other day and bought the CD on eBay.

Vic keeps thinking to himself I must get a hotel room. He also keeps thinking to himself why didn't I book a room in advance? For one thing the meeting date and time were uncertain. There is his condo in Laguna Niguel, but that might be too presumptuous. Maybe a spontaneous decision like this is what is meant to be.

In any case failure is not an option.

He realizes he needs to pee really bad. Talk about bad timing. Wait! The beach restrooms.

Relieved in more ways than one he impatiently waits for the light to change from red to green at PCH and Broadway Street. When the light finally changes Vic scurries across the intersection almost pushing the pedestrians in front of him to the side.

◦❀◦

Meanwhile back at the restaurant the waiter brings out their lunch orders of Caesar's Salads and steak and lobster enchiladas. "He had an emergency call he needed to make," Dulce tells the waiter voluntarily.

Dulce feels her intuition is telling her something. She puts the two twenty-dollar bills in her wallet and flags their waiter. "Please hold our table. I need to step away for a few minutes."

"No problem," he replies wondering if there is trouble brewing in paradise.

Dulce takes off her heels, puts them in her large ample purse and grabs the flats she had placed there and puts them on.

Dulce quickly exits the patio entrance and makes her way to the path overlooking the ocean reaching the gazebo directly behind a hotel. She pauses, catches her breath and positions herself at a vantage point above and near the stairs. She removes the small pair of high-powered binoculars from her purse and trains it on the intersection of PCH and Broadway Street below and begins scanning for Fontaine.

◦❀◦

Vic is practically jogging down Broadway Street now wondering why the other people on the sidewalk are being so laid back and impeding his forward momentum. His hat blows off necessitating he stop his forward progress. A gust of wind pushes it further away. Picking it up Vic begins jogging again.

Finally reaching his car he notices his meter is expired. Along with sucking in air because he is out of breath Vic breathes a sigh of relief. No parking ticket is tucked underneath his windshield wipers.

---

Dulce watches the intersection. There! There's Fontaine she mumbles to herself. She recognizes his hat. Why is he walking so fast? Maybe he really is concerned his meter has expired.

She puts down her binoculars mulling things over. Fontaine said he was going to his car to put more money in the parking meter. That makes sense, but he isn't in a rational frame of mine. Dulce realizes neither is she. What is he up to? Dulce has an epiphany. Fontaine is going to move his car and find a hotel room!

Dulce involuntarily smiles then laughs out loud. Putting the binoculars back up to her eyes again she patiently scans the intersection. If he moves his car, he might drive it onto PCH where most of the Laguna Beach hotels are located.

---

Vic immediately hops in his classic red Camaro, manages to do an illegal U-turn and heads back to PCH on Broadway.

---

Then Dulce sees it. A classic red Camaro is waiting to turn right onto PCH from Broadway Street.

---

"How much longer is this light going to last?" Vic is turning red in the face practically apoplectic. "I could take a shower and then a nap waiting for this light to change," he says to nobody.

Mercifully the red turns to green as he peels out onto PCH as fast as he can shifting over to the left lane then brakes causing his car to shudder and the guy in back of him to slam on his brakes almost rear ending his highly insured red classic Camaro. The hotel he wants is near the restaurant. It is in the perfect location.

Vic tries to turn left into the hotel parking lot against a double yellow line and he is holding up traffic. The driver behind him begins honking their horn. Vic's agitation is hitting full stride and he drives forward seeing a cross street coming up.

He could double-back and enter the hotel parking lot from the right, but he must return to the restaurant as soon as possible. He decides to take the opportunity and turn left from PCH onto Cliff Street and see if he can get lucky and get a parking space somewhere there.

Vic gets a turn arrow and turns left from PCH onto Cliff Street putting him not too far away from the hotel and restaurant. The hotel is less than a block from the restaurant. He's already driving drunk. Uh oh, a parking cop is issuing tickets. Come on, come on he repeats under his breath praying for a space.

Praise the Lord he sees somebody pulling out. Vic flicks his right turn signal on waiting for the car to exit causing the person behind him to wait. I'm glad I'm not that guy Vic thinks to himself as he pulls in. Adding icing to the cake there is still over an hour left on the meter. He pumps the meter up with quarters to the maximum amount.

◦⁂◦

Dulce's intuition and instincts are kicking in furiously. She is anticipating Fontaine will attempt to find a hotel near the restaurant. Doing an about face Dulce begins a slow trot along the path back to the restaurant.

As she is walking past the restaurant, she cranes her face to the right and sees their waiter taking an order on the outside patio. Walking around shrubbery she darts into the patio and runs up to him interrupting his order taking, impetuously takes one of Vic's twenty-dollar bill from her wallet and thrusts it into his hands.

"Keep my table free," she says as she hops over some shrubbery and scampers back to the path.

She sees a street that loops around in the distance. Fontaine might try parking there because maybe he won't be able to get a parking space at the nearby hotel on PCH. Dulce slows up and finds a vantage point that will allow her to spy on Fontaine undetected with her binoculars. She trains her binoculars. Dulce laughs because she realizes she is close enough not to need binoculars. All she needs to do is keep out of sight.

There it is. She would recognize that red classic Camaro anywhere. It's still a great looking car. Looks like there aren't any parking spaces to be had and making things worse a traffic cop is issuing tickets. Whoa! A car is pulling out. Fontaine got lucky.

Dulce waits for Fontaine to park and get of his car as she relocates to an even less detectable position. Now aware of her surroundings she notices a man painting on a canvass who is looking at her with a wary eye.

She watches as Fontaine, that is, Vic, walks back to PCH and goes to the right heading for the hotel just down the street. She stealthily follows him remaining a discreet distance behind him incognito as he walks down PCH, turns to the right and disappears into the hotel.

Dulce quickly does an about face and walks back to the restaurant and returns to their table. That was cute she thinks. Vic is cute. Cute is an understatement she decides as she puts her heels back on.

While she was doing her detective work Dulce sees Joaquin sent her a text. She sends him a reply text.

"Everything is under control. Your baby sister can take care of herself."

Dulce knows she might have a big decision to make later today. But Fontaine might not be able to get a room. You can't just walk into that hotel and get a room. Maybe you can at other hotels, but not at that hotel.

---

Vic walks into the small hotel lobby and approaches two clerks at the front desk. An eager to please young man greets him behind the counter. A young woman is working with another customer. Vic is grateful he got the guy.

"I'd like a room with a King size bed please," Vic says.

"May I please have your reservation number?"

"Why is it I need a reservation everywhere I go around here? Restaurants, hotels you even have to pay for the pleasure of parking your car. At least I can breathe the air without a reservation."

The front desk clerk picks up that this potential customer is upset. His customer service training takes over.

"We currently have no vacancies sir. Due to the popularity of the location of our hotel our rooms are typically booked weeks in advance. I apologize for any inconvenience. If you would like to make a reservation now for the future, I can do that for you."

"Good. I'd like a reservation for the future. Tonight."

The clerk can tell this is very important to this gentleman. Lowering his voice so his work colleague can't hear him and moving his head closer to Vic, the young man whispers, "Sir, why is it so important for you to get a room tonight?"

"I'm in love," Vic answers softly so the young woman behind the counter won't hear. "You can understand that. It has to be this hotel because it has to be. I'm asking you to accept that answer."

The young man turns to his computer monitor. After some clever clickity-clicks on the reservation terminal keyboard he says, "Sir, a room just became available. Room 323 with a beautiful ocean view off the balcony. Which credit card will we be using?"

"Thank you, thank you," Vic says with a hushed voice.

Vic hands the young man his AMEX card along with a hundred-dollar bill. He knew he'd be needing spreading around cash money today.

The front desk clerk gives Vic the key to Room 323 and a receipt and returns his AMEX card.

Vic departs the hotel lobby heading back to the restaurant.

※

Dulce sees it is half past two. Vic has been gone for an hour. She has finished eating her Caesar's Salad and steak and lobster enchiladas. The waiter has been very understanding. She keeps getting the feeling that she is under surveillance by the employees at the restaurant including the table bussers.

"I'm back," Vic thunders out startling Dulce as he takes his chair. "I see you finished lunch. I'm starved. I hope my food isn't too cold."

"Did you manage to find your car? You were gone an hour."

"I found my car. I'm paid up for several hours. You should make sure your car isn't running out of time too."

"I thought maybe you didn't remember where you parked your car and got lost." Dulce was doing her best not to break down laughing at his adorable antics. It was proving to be a challenge.

"I found it. I parked on Broadway. Where did you park?"

"In the public lot," Dulce says quick wittingly fabricating a falsehood. "Twenty dollar daily flat rate."

"I didn't know Laguna had a public lot. Then again I don't get over here much even though I live close by."

"Where do you live?" she asks wanting to know.

"Laguna Niguel," he replies knowing that nugget of information might impress her.

"Why did you choose Laguna Beach?"

"Because Lynn and I would come here once in a while and I remembered how beautiful it is. There is a lot of beauty to be seen in Laguna."

Dulce smiles to herself figuring that compliment was meant for her.

Their waiter shows up on schedule. "Please bring me another greyhound, a double this time. Bring the lady whatever she wants."

"I'll have a greyhound too," Dulce replied.

"You like greyhounds?" Vic asks, noticing how sexy that grey streak looks in Dulce's long flowing black hair.

"I just want to find out why you like them."

"It's a great drink. You'll like it."

The waiter returns with their greyhounds.

Vic, fortified by success, is embolden to say, "Honey, would like anything else to eat?"

Dulce looks up at the waiter.

"I'm still stuffed from the steak and lobster enchiladas. Still, do you have French toast? That and bagels with cream. That would be nice."

"Coming up," he says a large grin plastered on his face. "You'll need coffee with that."

"Yes, please. Thank you," Dulce replies noticing two restaurant staffers standing outside the door to the main dining area are making gestures at her and Vic.

Vic immediately drains half of his greyhound.

"You shouldn't drink so much on an empty stomach," Dulce councils as Vic begins to eat.

"I want to get drunk," Vic comments as he begins wolfing down his steak and lobster enchiladas. Dulce takes Vic's Caesar Salad without his permission.

"Why do you want to get drunk?" Dulce asks as she begin eating Vic's salad.

"I always like getting drunk on beautiful days surrounded by beautiful scenery," he saucily retorts.

"I think you drink because you are nervous and insecure."

"Thank you, Dr. Dulce, for that analysis. You sound like my therapist."

"You have a therapist?"
"I do. Thanks to you."
"Thanks to me?"
"Thanks to you."

Dulce takes a sip of her greyhound.

"Surprisingly good." She takes a second sip realizing how much she likes looking at Vic's profile thinking he is better looking than she remembered.

"Drink up," Vic says. "Eat, drink and be merry."

The waiter brings the French toast, bagels with cream and two coffees. He brings enough bagels and cream cheese to feed an army.

Dulce begins eating her French toast.

"That was the best meal I have ever had in my life," Vic concludes as he leans back after putting away his steak and lobster enchiladas.

"Tell me about your therapy Victor."

"About six months ago I started dreaming about you. Then the crying began."

Dulce interrupts Vic.

"I am sorry for the loss of your wife. It must be difficult to lose a lifelong partner."

Vic nods and begins tearing up.

"It is. Lynn was my best friend Dulce. I cheated on her when I gave you that perfume. I don't want to refloat that boat."

Vic begins weeping. She gets up and puts her arms around him.

She lays her head on the back of his head as his shoulders are shuddering with the sobs that are coming in waves.

The other customers sitting on the patio are taking notice. The waiter walks over swiftly.

"Is he okay?" the waiter asks with concern.

"He'll be fine, thank you," Dulce replies as Vic begins to recover.

Dulce slowly releases Vic and returns to her chair. She takes a stiff drink as he finishes his.

"I'm sorry," Vic sputters as he wipes away tears with his napkin.
"You have nothing to be sorry for Vic."
"I loved her so much. Now she's gone."

Dulce waves at the waiter who is hovering nearby on standby.

"Bring us both a double greyhound."

"You got it," he says as he hurries away on his mission of mercy.

Dulce's heart is going out to Vic. This man isn't a nut case. He is grieving for his wife and needs time to heal.

"I'll be back in a few minutes," Vic says as he goes to the men's room.

※

"I don't know about you, but I am drunk," Vic comments.

"I'm not feeling any pain," Dulce says as she stretches while biting into a bagel smeared with cream cheese. Joaquin has texted her three more times and she hasn't replied. He also called her twice his messages going to voice mail. Make that three phone calls he is calling again.

"Tell me about your therapy sessions," Dulce asks again.

"Hold that thought," Vic remarks as he flags down the waiter.

"What may I bring you?"

"A bottle of Jack Daniels Old No. 7 Tennessee Whiskey and two tumblers. You must have that. It was Frank Sinatra's favorite spirit."

Vic hands the waiter another twenty to grease the wheels.

"I'll be right back," he says. "Will you be staying for dinner?"

Vic and Dulce look at each other and start guffawing at the same time sensing this date or meeting of theirs will be a long day's journey into night.

"Bring us two menus," Dulce says after she recovers.

Dulce finishes her bagel. "I don't know I can squeeze any more food into my tummy," she says.

The waiter brings two menus, two tumblers and a bottle of Jack Daniels.

"That's what I'm talking about," Vic says appreciatively handing him a twenty forgetting he already gave the waiter a twenty a few minutes ago.

Dulce begins snickering. "Didn't you just – "
"Didn't I just what?"
"Never mind. Let's see what's for dinner."

"I'll give you two time to decide," the waiter says. He updates all of his coworkers on the couple sitting in the corner table outside on the patio.

"What you having?" Vic says looking at Dulce with adoration.
"Whatever you're having Vic," Dulce says, thinking Vic looks more distinguished now than he did twelve years ago.
"When I come here, I see food. Get it? I made a joke."

Dulce begins doubling over with laughter caused more by the alcohol in her body than any comedic skills exhibited by Vic.

"I should order seafood for me and something else for you and slip a shemp, I mean a shrimp, in your pasta. Shemp was one of The Three Stooges."
"Are you ordering pasta?" Dulce asks.
"I could. I should and I will. How about spaghetti?"
"Spaghetti works for me. If it works for you it works for me."

Vic bursts out laughing and does a high-five that Dulce meets halfway.

They are both legally drunk.

He pours the two tumblers with whiskey.

Vic leans into Dulce slurring his words.

"Now this is important. You gotta treat Mr. Daniels with respect. This is sippin' whiskey not tequila."

"You think because I'm of Mexican American heritage I automatically drink tequila?"

"Oh no, no, no, no, not at all. I was just saying."

"Glad we got that settled," Dulce says, erupting into laughter again.

Vic's first attempt at pouring is slightly off the mark. "I hate wasting Jack Daniels," Vic utters as the waiter arrives back at the table.

Seeing Vic's distress, he pours both tumblers.

"You are a squalor and a gentleman," Vic says. "Pardon me, I meant a scholar."

"May I take your orders now?"

"Soon as I explain to this fine lady the finer points of drinking whiskey. You see Dulce you put it to your lips like this."

Vic positions the tumbler on his lips looking deep into Dulce's eyes.

"Then you tilt the tumbler slightly and take a little bit and swish it around in your mouth before swallowing. Got it?"

"Got it."

Vic demonstrates and Dulce emulates him.

"It stings the tip of my tongue." Dulce carefully swallows. It's warm going down," she observes.

"Bravo, Bravo. That's funny. Did you get it? Your last name is Bravo and bravo can be a salutation. I think I remember Clint Eastwood saying it once in a movie. I'll make a whiskey drinker out of you yet."

Dulce is grinning while scrolling on her phone.

"Bravo is an exclamation meaning recognition when somebody does something well and the name of the movie you couldn't think of is 'For a Few Dollars More'."

"You are fast on the keyword searches Dulce," Vic says sincerely. "Did you already know the name of that movie Bravo, or did you find it online?"

Dulce ignores Vic's question.

Vic notices the waiter looming over him. "May I do something for you?"

"Yes. Give me your orders."

"Two big orders of spaghetti with lots of meatballs and sauce and parmesan cheese."

"Sir, if you'll notice spaghetti is not on tonight's menu. How about some pasta primavera?"

Vic begins laughing as does Dulce.

"Works for us," they both spontaneously and boisterously say attracting the attention of the other diners on the patio.

Their waiter smiles at their condition.

"Very good. Two orders of pasta primavera."

"You know what?" Vic says as the waiter walks away.
"What?" Dulce replies.
"We already had lunch. I think we just ordered lunch again. Or is that supposed to be dinner? I didn't talk about my therapy."
"Please do."

Vic puts down his tumbler.

"I have something on my mind."
"No kidding," Dulce says.
"You and I are strangers. Right? We do have an experience overlap by working at Johnson Industrial Supply and the events that occurred. I

suggest we tell each other the story of our lives. That way I can tell you the therapy later and it'll make more sense."

"That is the most sensible thing you've said all day Fontaine and you are wasted. Do you have to be wasted to be sensible?"

"Sometimes. Where to begin?"

"How about at the beginning Fontaine? I mean Vic. You are right Vic we are strangers. I don't know the first thing about you except you have a fetish for perfume, were on trial for laundering drug money and have incredible intuition. How you figured out 'The Sound of Music' was amazing."

Vic grins and takes a sip thinking Dulce is starting to like me. He launches into his Curriculum Vitae.

"I was born in Huntsville, Alabama on May 28, 1966. My life was pretty normal. I have one sister. I graduated from high school and went to college at the University of North Alabama and graduated in 1988 with a major in Accounting. That is where I met Lynn. She majored in Accounting too. I got a job in Peachtree City, Georgia working at the NCR Distribution Center in Logistics Accounting."

Vic takes a sip as Dulce asks a question.

"How did you end up in California?"

"I'm getting to that. Lynn had a miscarriage and we were told she couldn't have children. She and I decided to pursue her dream of being a dog groomer. Lynn was never into accounting although she was good at it. She was the bookkeeper for the business.

Around 1990 we used money from her mother's estate and opened a pet and dog grooming shop in a small retail area. Peachtree City is a nice town a planned community. That is where my road to California began."

"How so?" Dulce asks taking a slow sip herself.

She thinks of something. "I think we need to ease off on our drinking."

Vic, who had already lifted his tumbler halfway to his mouth, puts it down.

"You are wise sweetie," realizing he let 'sweetie' slip out. Then he has a vague feeling a 'honey' might have slipped out earlier as well. Instead of being embarrassed Vic smiles and laughs. Dulce smiles and laughs too.

"Any who," Vic begins as Dulce interrupts.

"Any who? Is that someone I'm supposed to know?" she says, then leans forward laughing.

"I meant anyway," Vic says.

"Anyway, like I said we opened a pet store and dog grooming parlor and things went well at first. What I didn't anticipate was the physical toll this was taking on Lynn."

Vic lifts his tumbler to his lips again as Dulce gives him a look and he places his tumbler back on the table as the waiter arrives with their orders of pasta primavera.

They begin lightly picking at their food both of them not hungry.

Vic picks up where he left off.

"The business was doing fine except the startup expenses required me to moonlight at a second job."

"What second job?"

"Cemetery sales. I worked four hours in the evening at a local cemetery overseeing two telephone solicitors. Business was always dead. We had a nice lay away plan."

Vic begins laughing hard as does Dulce. This continues for several minutes. Their waiter and other servers are watching them as their guffaws are attracting the attention of other diners on the patio and pedestrians strolling by on the path overlooking the ocean.

"Where was I?" Vic finally says. "I did the cemetery gig for a year. The extra money helped, but things were becoming unmanageable. It was burning me out working two jobs at the same time and Lynn and I didn't see each other except at night and on the weekends. That is when another health problem Lynn had showed itself."

Dulce sees that Vic is suddenly somber.

"Turns out she was what is called bipolar. It used to be called manic depression. I don't know if you know anything about what that is."

Dulce's jaw almost drops.

"My stepmom Camila was bipolar."
"Was bipolar? She passed away?"
"Yes."

Vic and Dulce look at each other with mutual understanding.

"Then you know what is involved. It was terrible. We had the pet store until 1992. That is when I joined the Army."

"You joined the Army?"
"I did. Lynn worked with a recruiter and in a weak moment I signed the dotted line."

Dulce sat back processing this information.

"Let me get this straight. You went from being an accountant at NCR and being a sales manager at a cemetery and a pet store owner to being in the military."

"That's about the size of it," Vic replies, taking a sip with no objection from Dulce.

They look at each other comfortably as the waiter appears.

"May I get you anything?"
Dulce speaks up.

"We're fine. We will be having dinner. Just bring us two cups of coffee please and we'll get the menus later."

"Very good," he replies.

"We're staying for dinner?" Vic asks innocently still fairly inebriated.

"We are," Dulce says with a slight smile on her face.
"Where was I?" he strains to recollect.
"You joined the Army like in 'Stripes'."
"'Stripes'?"
"The name of a movie. I saw it a few weeks ago."
"I'll have to check it out."

Joaquin calls Dulce. She decides on a different approach.

"Hi Joaquin. Everything is okay. Here, why don't you talk to Vic yourself. Hold on."

"Vic, my brother Joaquin is on the line. He is the one who thinks you are a nut case. Why don't you talk to him?"

Vic is eager to redeem himself.

"No problem."

Dulce hands her phone to Vic.

"*¿Qué pasa?*" Vic says in his best Spanish.
"How are you?" Joaquin asks warily.
"I'm doing just great. Your sister and I are having a lovely day together in charming Laguna Beach."

There is an uncomfortable pause.

"I'm not a nut case. *Me no loco.*"

Dulce leans in toward Vic and whispers. "Say, 'No estoy loco'."

"*No estoy loco,*" Vic says to Joaquin.

Another pause. Vic gets the distinct feeling that Joaquin doesn't wish to converse with him.

"Nice chatting with you Joaquin."

With no reply forthcoming Vic gives the phone back to Dulce.

"Everything is fine Joaquin. Thank you for calling."

"Your brother seems like a nice guy," Vic comments.
"He is. You were saying. The Army."
"Yes. I signed up for a two-year term of enlistment and came into the Army as an E-3 a Private First Class."
"You weren't an officer?"
"No. I enlisted."
"How old were you when you entered the Army?"
"26."
"You managed to get through basic training despite being older than many I presume?"
"Yes, I was older than most of the recruits. It was tough. I had basic training at Fort Jackson, South Carolina. I got lucky. I was stationed in Germany from 1992 to 1994."
"Why was that lucky?"

Just then the waiter returns with their coffee and dinner menus.

"Thank you," Dulce says, who has become their liaison to the waiter and staff.

"Are you ready to order?"

"Give us a raincheck. It could be awhile. We're talking."

"I see," he says flashing a grin as he walks away with their uneaten plates of pasta primavera.

Dulce turns to Vic who is taking a sip of his coffee.

"Why was it lucky you were stationed in Germany?"

"We wanted to go overseas. If you're going to do one two-year term of enlistment might as well do some traveling. I mean might as well live in a place you otherwise wouldn't have a chance to live in.

Being stationed in Germany was part of my enlistment contract. Thanks to Lynn. It wasn't luck it was by design. Lynn's mother was born in Munich, Germany and she married an American from Decatur Alabama, where Lynn was born. Her mother became a naturalized citizen. After her father died when Lynn entered UNA the same year as me in 1988 her mother returned to Munich."

Dulce nods in acknowledgement.

"Being in the Army was a great experience," Vic continues. "I was stationed in the city of Zweibrucken in the southwestern corner of Germany about 12 kilometers from the French border. I was in the Finance Directorate at the base.

I should tell you the story about how Lynn figured out we were being ripped off."

"Ripped off? What do you mean?" Dulce asks, curious.

"Well," Vic said, lifting his tumbler to his lips, then stopping midway looking at Dulce for sanction, who says, "Go ahead."

"Thank you," Vic says taking a conservative sip. Vic thinks to himself, 'Am I taking orders from her like she is my wife? Imagine that'.

"You were saying you were ripped off," Dulce prompts him as she takes a sip herself.

Vic continues.

"We rented the second floor of a three-story home owned by a guy named Arno Schmidt. I remember the day we rented the room the soldier who was leaving was there packing. I asked him how he liked the place and he said it's nice, and it was except for the misplaced bathroom in the stairwell.

He said the Schmidts were nice and he told me as an afterthought something like, 'I'm leaving the Army when I return to the states and I have been trying to save money and my utility bill keeps going up and up'.

I didn't think about his comment to me until a couple months later when I noticed the same thing even though Lynn and I were conservative in our use of electricity.

Lynn was showing signs of going into mania and on a Sunday when the Schmidts were out of the house she tells me, 'I figured out how the Schmidts are ripping us off. You must go down to the basement with me'. I'm thinking, 'Yeah right', because I knew she was getting sick and I was worried the Schmidts would come home and find us snooping around down in their basement.

Lynn kept after me and after me so I relented. We go down the stairs from the Schmidt's living room and enter their basement where they had a washer and a dryer. Three electrical meters are hanging on the wall stacked and labeled 1, 2 and 3. She told me, 'See our number 2 meter how it is turning?' The second meter's dial was turning while the first and third floor meters were not moving at all. She says something like, 'Watch'.

Lynn turns on the washer and dryer and the second meter begins turning even faster. I'm looking at it and I can't believe what I'm seeing. I told her, 'Turn them off'. The second-floor meter started turning slower.

We tried it a couple more times and it was clear the electricity for the washer and dryer and for the whole house was shunted into the second-floor meter.

All electricity in the three-story house was being shunted to the second room electric meter in the basement so his American tenants including Lynn and me paid the electric bill for the Arno Schmidt's entire house.

I was angry to say the least. When Schmidt and his wife and whoever the other person was got home I confronted him at the front door and I said to him in German, '*Herr Schmidt, Ich weiss, dass irgendwas da unten stimmt was nicht*', which means 'Mr. Schmidt, I know something fishy is going on downstairs'."

"You speak German?" Dulce asks.

"A little. I had rehearsed that line and the German might not be grammatically correct. Lynn could speak passable German and she coached me. Then I told him in English, 'I know you have been ripping me off and all of the Americans who have lived here. Lynn found out'. He was so shocked he said in his broken English, 'This is the first time in twenty years anyone figured it out'.

I wanted to beat the stuffing out of him. Lynn and I moved out.

Arno and I had gotten into a habit of sharing a beer together now and then. I don't know why he had to steal from us. It took my sleuth Lynn to uncover his scam. After Lynn uncovered Arno Schmidt's scam, I reported him to the commanding officer of my unit.

You know what I was told? 'We have to maintain good relations with the local community'.

He didn't care after all I was only an E-5 Sergeant and one month later I found out Schmidt had rented out the middle floor in his house again to another American. That hurt too."

Vic finishes his coffee as he gets a refill.

"Are you ready to order yet?" the waiter asks.

"Tell you what," Dulce says, "Come back in an hour."

Vic takes a twenty from his wallet and hands it off to the waiter, who accepts it and walks away without comment.

"How many twenties have you given him?" Dulce asks.

"Not as many as I gave the hotel clerk. Wait, I didn't give him twenties. I gave him a C-Note," Vic answers, who turns red and laughs his Jack Daniels keeping him fortified and uninhibited.

"Loose lips sink ships," Vic mutters looking at Dulce. He blurts out laughing once more feeling no pain.

She smiles back and smoothly returns to the subject at hand.

"You and Lynn moved to another rental?"

"Yeah. What was it I going to tell you related to California?" Vic asks trying to recall.

"You were going to tell me how you ended up in California. Please go on."

"How that happened was about six months before I was scheduled to leave Germany and return to the states, I began going to the base library a couple times a week and reading the Help Wanted and Want Ad sections of all of the newspapers on their newspaper sticks. This was before the internet started becoming the most common way to find a job.

I was looking for accounting and other business type positions. I was disciplined and determined. I had to be otherwise I would be returning home from the Army to my parent's home in Huntsville without any job prospects waiting for me.

I mailed out over 800 resumes the last month I was stationed at Zweibrucken. I used a local printer to print the resumes. My parent's address in Huntsville was the return address.

When Lynn and I returned, we stayed at my parent's house like I told you. I received over two hundred replies to my resume letters. One came from McDonnell Douglas in Monrovia. They offered to fly me out for an interview. I flew into LAX and I remember being intimidated driving on the freeways and groping my way along trying to find the correct offramp to Monrovia.

I interviewed and flew back home. A few days later they called me with an offer and I accepted. Lynn and I drove out to California and the rest is history."

"What year was this?" Dulce asks, trying not to appear too eager to find out about Vic's life story. She realizes he is buzzed and isn't especially alert to those nuances.

He takes another sip after she gives him permission to do so.

"1994 I think," Vic finally replies his speech slightly slurred. "Let me see. Yep, 1994 because the year I was discharged, honorably discharged mind you, from the Army and the year I got the job in Monrovia, California."

"You went from Germany to Alabama to California in one fell swoop. What happened next?"

"Everything was rolling along until 1997 when Boeing bought out McDonnell Douglas. The McDonnell Douglas plant was transferred to El Paso. I was fortunate enough to land a position at Boeing in Huntington Beach. This was 1998.

They had more consolidations buying out the space part of North American Rockwell. I worked there from 1998 to mid-2004 when I was laid off. Parts of 2004 and 2005 were two of the worst years of my life besides last year. I was out of work for eleven months and my unemployment only lasted three months. As you might remember in mid-2005, I started working at Johnson."

"Where were you and Lynn living at the time?"

"Pasadena. That was a long commute driving back and forth from Pasadena to my job in Huntington Beach every day."

"What happened next?" Dulce asks, doing her best not to seem as interested as she is. She is enjoying Vic's pedantic parade down memory lane and it is providing her with interesting information to help her size him up.

"I kept looking for a job. Jobs in aerospace were hard to come by at that time. I had one promising bite from an industrial supply company in Santa Fe Springs. I can't remember their name it's on the tip of my tongue. I should be able to remember it. If I heard the name of the company, I'd recognize it. I had two interviews with them and was even shown the desk where I would work. The phone rang on our land line and Lynn, who was not well, grabbed the phone before I could answer it.

She talked gibberish and I yanked the phone out of her hand. It was someone from that company who I know in my gut was calling to offer me a job. They got off the phone quickly. I knew any chance I had to work for them was over. Lynn squashed the deal for me. That was frustrating."

Vic pours himself a drink and guzzles it down halfway without dissent from Dulce and continues talking.

"Just before I was hired at Johnson, Lynn and I were two or three weeks away from being homeless. Lynn had spent weeks in psychiatric hospitals for bipolar disorder and I was staying in bad motels desperately looking for a job."

"Is Lynn's bipolar condition why you developed an interest in Eric Berne and intuition?"

"No. Lynn was the one who got me interested. She believed in the power of intuition long before I did. What I mean is she was a fan of Eric Berne long before I was."

"Interesting," Dulce said, taking a long sip, then pouring herself a refill of Tennessee Whisky, wondering about that company in Santa Fe Springs. Could it be the company she thinks it might be? The company she works for now Kim's Business Supplies? She decides to put it on the shelf for now and listen.

"When I was hired at Johnson, I was probably suffering from PTSD. Then came you."

Vic finished his drink and poured himself another tumbler full.

"You should ease off Victor," Dulce says.

"I will," Vic replied after taking a long sip.

"We've talked enough about me. Let's push the pause button where I was hired at Johnson and you tell me about you," he says emphatically.

Dulce takes a sip and then another and starts talking.

"It's a deal. I'll start at the beginning like you did. I was born on March 2, 1976 in Montebello. Like you my life was pretty normal. I have two brothers and one sister. I graduated from high school in 1994 and worked part-time at a coffee shop while I attended Pasadena City College. My daughter Sophia was born in 1996 and I dropped out of PCC to care for her."

"What did you major in?" Vic inquires starring at Dulce.

"My major was Data Entry and Microcomputer Applications. I eventually graduated. I'll get to that later. I got a job in Order Entry at Johnson in 1997. Some of the things I learned at PCC paid off in my job."

"You'd already been working at Johnson for eight years before I came on board in 2005," Vic interjects.

"That's right Sherlock," Dulce responds.

Vic begins laughing, then asks rhetorically, "Why am I laughing?" Then he laughs again.

"You called me Sherlock. Do you read Sherlock Holmes mysteries?"

Dulce doesn't answer and resumes her life story.

"Camila wasn't in good mental health at the time and her insurance premiums were COBRA because she had lost her job a few months earlier. My dad was on disability receiving SSI. I was chipping in to cover her health premiums with my brothers Joaquin and Gustavo.

My sister Consuelo was taking care of Sophia and Camila while I worked. Camila felt bad about us paying for her health insurance and somehow managed to acquire a part-time job as a security guard."

"Don't you have to have some kind of what you call it certification to be a security guard?" Vic asks after a loud burp.

"Yes, a guard card. We still don't know how she was able to get one."

Vic burps again. "Sorry."

Dulce reaches over and takes Vic's tumbler away and places it in the center of the table.

"What do you think you're doing?" Vic says with indignation.

"Keeping you from passing out. How much have you had to drink today?"

"Almost as much as you."

"I see your point," Dulce concedes.

Vic reaches over and takes Dulce's tumbler away and puts it next to his tumbler in the center of the table.

"You were saying something about your stepmother Camila being a security guard."

Dulce resumes her story.

"Camila managed to get hired by a security guard company as an unarmed guard. She had a uniform. She must have somehow managed to take a taxi to be interviewed if that is how she was hired. Consuelo saw her in her uniform going out the door to a cab. That was the day she was on assignment to work at Johnson."

"Our Johnson?" Vic slurs being overtaken by the high level of alcohol cruising through his body and brain despite having temporarily stopped imbibing.

"Our Johnson," Dulce verifies. "The one and only."

Vic is gazing at Dulce intently observing her facial expressions and how precious they are.

"I entered the front lobby and the security guard sitting at the desk looked familiar. Then my stepmother yells out, 'Dulce'! Imagine my surprise when I saw my stepmother sitting in that guard chair. I said something like 'What are you doing here'?

I couldn't linger because other people were coming into the lobby and I didn't want anyone to know my stepmother was the guard. I clocked in and was hoping everything would be alright. I was thinking that she must be somewhat normal or else the guard company wouldn't have sent her out on assignment to Johnson.

A couple hours passed. I checked in on her a few times and all seemed to be well. She was sitting quietly at the guard desk checking employee ID badges and logging visitors in. I know she had been taking her meds regularly at the time because Consuelo was good at making sure of that. I began to relax believing that everything was going to be fine.

I was in a meeting when Lucia interrupts and asked to see me privately. I stepped outside the conference room and Lucia tells me a lady wearing a security guard uniform is being disruptive in the front lobby telling everyone that her stepdaughter Dulce works at Johnson and owns the company.

Lucia wanted to know if that woman really was my stepmother and I told her yes. Lucia then asked me to go calm her down or else they would have to call the police. My stepmom Camila had rifled through the mail slots in the mail room and tossed the mail on the floor. The Johnson mail room has a memory burn for me in more ways than one.

I rushed to the front lobby and she was creating an uproar locking the front lobby door preventing some important visitors from coming in and just causing a mess. It was bad. I couldn't calm her down. It was embarrassing. Lucia called 911 and Camila was eventually taken to Las Encinas Hospital in Pasadena and placed on a 72-hour psychiatric hold."

"A 5250," Vic commented. "That's a code for a mental health call. I know the drill. Lynn was hospitalized at Las Encinas more than once. It's a great hospital. Great food in the dining area."

"It is a great hospital," Dulce says, smiling at Vic. He understands. "Yes, the food is excellent. She ended up staying there about a month and was discharged. I am grateful California considered mental health on par with physical health as far as insurance is concerned way before other states did. Her insurance paid for her stay. That is why it was so important we kept up her COBRA payments."

Dulce pauses looking at Vic feeling a bond developing between them.

"Did Camila stay in one of the cabins out back?" Vic asks.

"She did. I know the cabins have names I don't remember the name of the one she was in. I remember visiting her and then walking around outside with her. It is very peaceful. "

"Maybe Lynn and Camila were at Las Encinas at the same time," Vic speculates.
"Could be," Dulce agrees.
"Who knows, we might have seen each other there."
"It's possible," she concurs.

Dulce began to reminisce.

"I know that scene at work hurt my chances for a promotion at Johnson. That was one reason I eventually left the company."

"When did this scene take place?" Vic asks, feeling empathetic. "It must have been before I was hired at Johnson in 2005."

"Sometime in 2004. About a year before you came on board."
"I can honestly say I understand," he comments.

Dulce smiles at Vic knowing he understands.

"Tell me about going to PCC," Vic requests.

Dulce almost takes a sip, realizing she would rather be drinking red wine instead of whisky.

"Like I said I my major was Data Entry and Microcomputer Applications. I finally got my degree in 2001 going to school part time. I had to drive straight from work in Commerce to Pasadena on nights I had classes."

"What kind of classes did you take?" he wants to know.
Dulce begins a nervous laugh.
"I almost failed one class."
"You did?"

"I did. It was a final exam in spreadsheets. We had to take ten different business situations in order and build our spreadsheets. It was a two-hour final and I was doing well. I got to the last step of the exam the tenth step and input my data. I was very proud of what I did. I logged out and turned in my reference notes and thumb drive to the instructor. There was only one problem. Care to guess what it was?"

"I can't guess. What happened?"
"I didn't save my work."
"Didn't save your work? That was the reason you almost failed this class? You've got to be kidding me."
"No, I'm not. At first the professor wasn't going to cut me any slack. I almost had to take the class again."

Vic feels anger rising up within him.

"If I had been your husband or boyfriend, I would have paid that professor a visit."

"Hello! Didn't you hear the part where I said I almost had to take the class again? I said almost. I had to stay late and redo the final step of the exam. That time I saved the file and passed the final. It learned a good lesson. I never forgot it. What's this if you had been my husband or boyfriend?"

"That was just a figure of speech," Vic replies, taking a long sip and refilling his tumbler with whiskey again.

"I'm sure it was," Dulce says.

"What other classes did you take?" He asks.
"I don't want to talk about my other classes. The important thing is I graduated."
"I'm proud of you," Vic announces.
"I'm sure you are," she responds, smiling imperceptibly.
"Sophia is going to PCC," Dulce mentions.
"What is she studying?"
"I think it's called Design Technology or CAD Designer. She wants to be an architect."
"She sounds smart, like her mom."

Vic takes a sip and thinks he is being too obvious and too free with his compliments. Dulce doesn't seem to be minding. In his inebriated state it is difficult for him to tell. It would be difficult for him to tell if he was completely sober too.

"I have some issues," Vic mentions without embarrassment. "I know that's not something you discuss on your first date."

"We're not on a date. This is a meeting. You called it a meeting in your email. If anything, it was a date to have a meeting."

"Meeting?" Vic snorts. "It feels like a date to me and my intuition is right more often than not. Remember you were the one who said I have amazing intuition."

"For that one-off event only," Dulce replies defensively.

"Oh yeah? I'll have you know I have other examples of my amazing intuition."

"You and your intuition," Dulce says in annoyance wishing she hadn't told Vic he has amazing intuition.

"My batting average is better than Ted Williams."

"Oh please," Dulce says derisively as she can trying to sound authentic. "You play in the minor leagues."

"Are we having our first fight?" Vic wonders out loud.

"We had our first fight when you put the Dulce Bravo perfume in my mail box at work."

Vic studies Dulce taking in her expressive mannerisms, which he finds captivating, charming and exponentially fascinating. Everything about her is fascinating he thinks.

Their waiter strides towards them.

"Are you ready to order yet?" the waiter asks Dulce one more time.

"Tell you what," Dulce says to the waiter, "Come back in an hour."

"That's what you said an hour ago," he fires back.

Vic takes a twenty from his wallet and gives it to the waiter, who gets the hint and departs.

"Your life Dulce. Tell me more about your life."

"You want some more war stories?"

"Sounds like a plan."

"Okay. There was the time I slid into home while playing softball and hurt my right knee."

"You played baseball?"

"Softball. When I was ten."

"What happened?"

Dulce takes a small sip of her Jack Daniels as Vic takes the bottle and begins to pour whiskey into Dulce's tumbler.

"No," Dulce says as she waves Vic off.

"You sure?" Vic says with disappointment in his voice as he refreshes his tumbler.

"Yes. Back to softball."

"Like a Ferengi on Star Trek I'm all ears."

Dulce tries not to laugh. She is a Star Trek fan and comprehends Vic's reference to the Ferengi.

"I had made it to third base and the next batter hit a single. I don't remember what the score was, but the home base couch was waving me in. I slid and my right knee caught the corner of home plate that was curled upward.

I felt a sharp stabbing pain and the right leg of my white uniform was covered in red. People were running around looking for something to wrap around my knee. I was taken to the hospital and stitched up. I had to use a cane at school for a couple of weeks. I have a scar."

"May I see it?" Vic asks without unease.

Dulce turns her chair toward Vic and sticks out her right leg as Vic moves his chair closer.

He leans forward as Dulce points to a small spot of skin with slight discoloration just under her right knee.

"See it?"

"I see," Vic says not fully focused on the scar tissue on her knee.

Dulce withdraws her leg as Vic reluctantly scoots his chair back to its original position another memory burn forming.

"Are you a Dodgers fan?" he asks.

"Angels fan," she replies. "But I follow the Dodgers too."

Vic remembers a sports related story of his own.

"For a semester of seventh grade I was Tree Man."

"Tree Man?" Dulce asks incredulously.

"Tree Man!" Vic utters with emphasis.

Dulce snickers.

"I was running to catch a football pass and I ran into a tree in my neighbor's front yard. When I collided with the tree I bounced back and ended up on my back dazed."

"Did it hurt?" Dulce asks.

"I don't remember any pain. I remember being dazed. I told my friend I needed to go home. Then I did something really dumb."

"Dumber than running into a tree?" Dulce says laughing unable to contain herself. She quickly recovers and waits as Vic takes a long sip.

"I mowed the lawn. I had postponed it and I knew my dad would be upset if he got home from work and found I hadn't done it yet. It was a hot day but I mowed the lawn. I remember going inside the house and standing in the hallway looking at myself in the mirror when the right side of my face began to swell up. My right eye was practically covered. My dad got home and I went to the emergency room and an x-ray showed I didn't have a skull fracture.

I dreaded going to school because I knew what was coming.

Being called Tree Man started when everyone asked me, 'How did it happen?' and I told them, 'I ran into a tree trying to catch a football pass'. There was a bully on the bus who started calling me Tree Man and it stuck. Kids can sure be mean. I couldn't shake being Tree Man for months."

Dulce and Vic look at each for a minute.

"How is your mother, your stepmother, I mean how is Camila doing?" Vic asks.

"Camila died of lung cancer," Dulce says slowly after a minute.

"I'm sorry," Vic replies in sympathy. "I forgot that you'd already told me she had passed away."

"My real mother died of breast cancer when I was very young," Dulce continues. "My real mother and my stepmother both died of cancer. I didn't know my real mother. Despite her bipolar illness Camila and I were close. I guess you could say Camila was my real mother."

Dulce and Vic are pensive and lost in thought.

"My wife Lynn died of pneumonia," Vic mentions.

"I know you told me that already. I'm sorry," Dulce replies in sympathy again

"Lynn had health problems the last five years of her life. She was battling type 1 diabetes and suffered from bronchitis since she was a child. Her bronchitis caused her to miss half of first grade when she was six. On top of all that she took meds for her bipolar."

Vic raises his tumbler to his lips, then puts it down without drinking anything. He remembers something he had been thinking about this morning driving to Laguna Beach.

"I told you my therapist told me I was suffering morbid grief due to Lynn's death and was experiencing PTSD. She also told me in her opinion I was also exhibiting symptoms of what is called hypomania, but she couldn't definitively give me a firm diagnosis without more sessions. I think a psychiatrist has to make a formal determination and diagnosis, but I'm not sure."

Dulce is searching for hypomania on her smart phone and finds it and reads about it as Vic is talking.

"It was during a bout of probable hypomania that I bought my 1967 classic red Camaro."

"Probable hypomania Fontaine?" she interrupts.

"Like I told you Bravo I've never been formally or officially determined to have hypomania.

I wouldn't have bought the Camaro under normal circumstances. I paid the price for buying it in many ways. I made significant sacrifices and I can honestly say I'm proud to own it. My therapist told me I suffer from anxiety."

"Anxiety Fontaine? How does that square with you giving me that bottle of perfume and those emails you sent me and the card you sent me and badgering me to meet with you here today after letting the whole world know how you feel about me?"

"I told you. Hypomania."

"Like I am supposed to know what that is? Are you sure you aren't using that as an excuse for your bad behavior?"

Vic considers the question and declines to answer silently invoking his fifth amendment rights against self-incrimination. He has pondered that question himself on occasion and doesn't have an answer.

"That is what you are googling, isn't it? What are you searching for? Are you googling hypomania?" he asks.

Dulce puts her phone down feeling agitated and annoyed for unknown reasons. She suddenly realizes she'd come across the term hypomania before related to her experiences with Camila.

"You should have known something was wrong with me when I put that perfume in your box and taken pity on me," Vic says in a confrontational tone.

"Pity on you? Did you want me to throw you a pity party? Are you a wimp?" she taunts.

"Pity is underrated and so is being a wimp. You could have been nice about it," he fumes

"Nice? How would you feel if I had put a bottle of Vic Fontaine cologne in your mail box?" she fumes back.

"I would have been flattered. I certainly wouldn't have gone complaining and singing the blues to Human Resources about it. You could have accepted my gift offer of expensive perfume instead of putting it in my mail slot. Imagine how embarrassed I was at your rejection."

"Now you're talking trash Fontaine. You're shuckin' and jivin'. Nothing but shuck and jive BS. When you put that perfume in my mail slot it was a disgusting display of impropriety. You were unfaithful to your wife. How did you even know there was such a thing as Dulce Bravo perfume?"

"That's another story," Vic replies, remembering it was an English pen pal of his who had clued him in on Dulce Bravo perfume after Vic regaled him with his tale of woe regarding the real Dulce Bravo.

Vic is getting his dander up and is building up a head of steam.

"That was a mean thing you said about my being unfaithful to my wife," Vic says with hostility. "I explained my regrets to you already and how bad it made me feel. Don't you think I know I was unfaithful to her when I put that damned perfume in your mail slot?

I knew I was on thin ice with you Bravo then and I know I am on thin ice with you now. I knew I shouldn't have sent those emails to Marisol. You and I have nothing in common. We can't be on the same page. I don't know why I wasted my time."

Dulce stares at Vic wondering why she's bothered spending one minute of her time mulling over whether to meet with him or not much less actually meeting with him. He has conceit and hubris and bombast in abundance. A first-class jerk who covers up his insecurities with banal trivialities.

Who in their right mind tries to contact someone they haven't seen in twelve years to restart a relationship that was never a relationship to begin with? His emails were off the wall with the incessant 'I love you' pledges and his corny Valentine's Day card. The whole thing is patently ludicrous and ridiculous.

Then she belatedly remembers all of that wasn't enough to keep her from meeting with Fontaine and purges that thought from her conscious mind.

He was unfaithful to his wife, though she admits he exhibited contrition and cried about it maybe she was over the top to mention it. It might have been unkind to rub it in his face.

Joaquin could be right. Maybe Fontaine is a nut job. According to Wikipedia hypomania could mean Vic suffers from a form of bipolar disorder if he really suffers from hypomania. That might explain how he got caught up in that drug trial. To top it off his late wife Lynn had bipolar disorder. Fontaine could be a hardened criminal at heart who simply got lucky and evaded justice.

In a moment of hasty uncertainty, heavily seasoned with residual generalized anger from the catalyst of their long ago partially toxic past non-relationship, Dulce stands up, grabs her purse and walks into the inside the restaurant through the main dining room and exits outside the restaurant onto Cliff Street.

Vic isn't so cute after all she thinks. Who ever heard of a cute criminal who is also a nut job? If this true she thinks to herself, then why does she want him to follow her?

Dulce is a mass of conflicting emotions.

When the waiter and staff see Dulce get up from her chair in a huff and rush through the restaurant and leave, he yells out to Vic, "Don't just sit there go follow her! Go get her and bring her back!"

The rest of the staff begins chanting at Vic, "Bring her back! Bring her back! Bring her back! Bring her back!"

Vic stands up and stumbles over the chair in front of him his blood alcohol content compromising his coordination, recovers and dashes through the restaurant after Dulce as the patrons watch the hubbub.

The waiter signals Vic and points to the front door.

Vic hurries outside and turns his head to the left and then to the right and spots Dulce walking toward PCH. He starts off at a trot and accelerates his pace to catch up with her before she reaches PCH.

"Dulce! Dulce! Hold up! Hold Up!" Vic shouts.

He catches up to her. She is almost at PCH.

"Dulce, come back to the restaurant," he says, slightly winded from his sprint. The muscle pull in his lower back hurts badly now.

Vic grabs her left forearm as she initially resists then relaxes as Vic tightens his grip.

Dulce looks at Vic's earnest face and backpedals. "Might as well not let good food go to waste," she says. She thinks to herself there is something appealing in the way he is gripping my forearm so tightly. Dulce is secretly happy that Vic came after her. She had expected nothing less from him and would have been crushed if he had let her go on her way without coming after her.

Vic turns Dulce around still holding her forearm firmly. They begin walking back to the restaurant. "Vic, I shouldn't have mentioned your wife in my rant," she says. Vic looks at her lovingly. "Dulce, I said things to you I shouldn't have said in my rant. We have much in common and we are on the same page."

He releases her forearm just before they reach the restaurant.

As Dulce and Vic enter the front entrance their waiter, the staff and everyone dining in the main dining room applaud loudly with somebody adding a whistle to the accolades. As they make their way back out to the patio and their table everyone sitting on the patio also breaks out into applause.

"I think we are having our fifteen minutes of fame," Vic says grinning as Dulce grins back.

They begin to giggle uncontrollably.
Dulce and Vic keep looking at each other giggling.

"Why are we giggling?" Dulce asks.
"We're not giggling," Vic protests. "We're laughing."
"I say we're giggling," Dulce replies between giggles.
"Tell you what," Dulce says, "I'll bet you I can look up the definitions of giggling and laughing and prove you wrong."
"I'll take that bet," Vic says smugly through his own giggles.

Dulce goes online on her phone.

"Here it is. Check this out Fontaine you owe me dinner. When used as verbs, giggle means to laugh gently or in a high-pitched voice, whereas laugh means to make sounds and movements of the face and body of instinctive expressions of lively amusement blah blah blah."

"What do you mean blah, blah blah?" Vic asks suspiciously. "Are you covering up something with your blahs?"
"No!" Dulce forcefully responds.
"But you used the word laugh in defining giggle. Tell you what, forget it. I lost the bet even though you only gave me the difference between the verbs, not the nouns, but the verbs giggle and laugh."
Dulce and Vic begin giggling again.

"I have many memory burns of you at Johnson," Vic states switching gears.
"Memory burns? Sounds like a medical condition like hypomania. Or the name of a movie star."
"What I mean is there were certain things or certain times when I was observing you that permanently stuck in my mind."

Dulce lifts her tumbler to her lips taking a very slight sip of Jack Daniels Old Number 7 Whiskey.

"Name some," Dulce taunts.

"Alright, I just might. Let me see, where to begin. I have several."
"Take them in order of their occurrence," Dulce suggests.

Dulce takes another sip and Vic drains his tumbler.

"There's the time you were organizing your desk. You were very proud."
"Proud of organizing my desk?"
"May I be allowed to speak without interruption?"
"Okay," Dulce allows. "Let's hear it. I'll permit you to speak without interruption."

"That's more like it," Vic says continuing, then he decides to qualify that remark.
"Allow me to rephrase. It's very gracious of you to permit me to speak without interruption."
"You're welcome," Dulce responds.

"I just happened to be checking something out in an empty cubicle behind yours and I heard you talking to one of the Customer Service reps I can't recall who. You were telling her how you had taken a section of the top of your desk and over the course of several days you had reorganized it. You went into detail what you did on each day. That was like super cute. It was like cute on steroids."

"You were eavesdropping on me?" Dulce says in mock shock.
"Not intentionally it just so happened."
"What else you got?"
"Don't you remember organizing the top of your desk?"
"No. What else you got?"

Vic refills his tumbler with more whiskey.

"There was the time I was working in Purchasing on temporary assignment. What was her name the Purchasing Manager?"

"Francesca."

"Right Francesca. I don't know exactly what I was specifically doing, but I was sitting on the floor in the hallway outside of Francesca's office organizing some purchasing documents and you walked up. You and Francesca were going to lunch. You planted your right foot a few inches from my right hand. I looked up and you were standing over me and I gotta tell ya that was super sexy. It was more than sexy, it ah, it made me feel – "

"Submissive?" Dulce finishes the sentence for him.

"No. No! Absolutely not!" Vic resolutely protests as in you 'doth protest too much'. "I would not use that word," Vic argues. "It was just somehow sexy and that is all I meant."

"I understand," Dulce says flashing a wicked grin. "Maybe something like you wanted me to put a dog collar on you and lead you around with a chain."

"I bet you would have loved to tell me to 'Sit Vic' like I was a dog."

"You would have submitted to obedience like a good dog Vic."

Vic looks intently at Dulce that memory burn churning in his brain.

"I do remember that happening," Dulce says after a pause in the repartee.

"Really?"

"Really. Get real Fontaine you were sitting on the floor in the hallway. You looked like a clown sitting on the floor with all those thick piles of rubber banded paperwork scattered everywhere. How could I not remember?"

Dulce knows there is more to why she remembered the event than she is letting on. Standing over Vic gave her a strange titillation providing her with a memory burn of her own.

"What else?" Dulce says, trying her best not to giggle.

"I hadn't been with Johnson too long and I needed help with Spanish. I saw you sitting there and just chose you randomly to help me translate something from English to Spanish. You were extremely helpful. I mean you jumped into action. That was nice."

"That must have been before the perfume incident," Dulce remarks not remembering this translation event.

"It was. There was the time you were telling somebody about a soccer match Sophia had been in. You were a very proud mom. I think Sophia scored a goal that won the game."

Dulce warmly recalls her time as the coach of Sophia's soccer team when Sophia was in elementary school.

"Go on," Dulce quietly says to Vic.

"This one involves Sophia too. One day you were putting flyers in the mail slots in the mail room and Mr. Johnson observed you. He was pissed and told me to write you up for distributing private literature for personal gain during working hours. I think it was a solicitation request to buy chocolate bars for Sophia's soccer team. I was really mad at Johnson and I felt sorry for you."

Dulce nods in recollection. That was petty of Johnson.

"That mail room was an unlucky place for us," Vic concludes. Dulce remains mute.

"There was the perfume incident, or caper as I like to call it. Let me circle back to that at the end. I have one more. This one was after the perfume caper. It was the second time I was called into Lucia's HR office. Do you remember that?"

Dulce nods her head affirmatively.

"If you remember Dulce you accused me of staring at you. I wasn't staring at you. I was staring at your legs."

"My legs? I think that deserves an explanation. I remember you staring at me. I remember filing a complaint with Lucia."

"You know where you used to sit. I just gotten some coffee in the copier room and was about to exit when I slowed down because I was walking fast and the coffee was spilling out of my cup. As I reached the exit you had your legs crossed and yes, I plead no contest to checking them out. What was I supposed to do? How did you see me anyway? I couldn't see your face. All that was in my line of sight were your lovely legs."

"I saw you checking my legs out this morning when I showed you my scar under my knee."

"Are you going to file another complaint?" Vic blubbers, then explodes in laughter as Dulce joins him.

"I'll let it go this time," Dulce says gasping for air because she was laughing so hard.

"Praise the Lord!" Vic preaches.

"Seriously, how did you see me looking at your legs?"

"I leaned over to scratch my leg and I saw you for a couple of seconds staring at me."

"But for an itch you wouldn't have seen me?"

"That's right. I think your memory burns are an indicator that you were stalking me at work."

Seeing a hurt look flash across Vic's face she qualifies, "I'm just messing with you Victor. Fontaine."

"Why can't you make up your mind whether to call me Vic, Victor or Fontaine?"

"I don't know. Is it because I am intoxicated?"

"That's a big part of it. If it makes you feel any better Bravo, I am intoxicated too."

Vic picks up his tumbler with as much flare as he can muster.

"I propose a toast. To intoxication."

"To intoxication," Dulce repeats, clicking her tumbler against Vic's tumbler.

They both begin to laugh uproariously.

"What happened when Lucia hauled you into her office for the second time?" Dulce asks.

Vic is staring at the table cloth.

"Earth to Vic, come in please. What happened when Lucia called you in for looking at my legs?"

"Oh," he replies. "She uh, well, Lucia read me the riot act. My defense was something like, 'I wasn't looking at Dulce I was looking at her legs,' or something like that."

"That's what you told her?" Dulce says beginning to crack up.

"I'm pretty sure that's what I told her."

Dulce and Vic click their tumblers one more time.

"Back to the perfume caper," Vic says, feeling giddy.

"You asked me earlier how I found out there was such a thing as Dulce Bravo perfume."

"Yeah Fontaine what's up with that?"

"You see my dear, I had a pen pal who lived in England."

"How did you have a pen pal in England?"

"I don't remember exactly. I think we met on one of those military gaming websites."

"You're a gamer?"

"There's lots you don't know about me sweetheart," Vic replies uninhibitedly.

Dulce scrutinizes Vic closely.

"You were saying you got to know this English chap somehow."

"Yes, I did Ms. Bravo. And during one of our email exchanges I told him all about you that I was crazy about you. When he asked me what your name was, I told him Dulce Bravo. You wanna know what he said then?"

"What?"

"He said, 'It's a small world. My brother is a salesman for Dulce Bravo perfume.' And I said, 'If you could send me a bottle of that perfume that would be a perfect gift'."

"Did he know you were married?" Dulce pointedly asks.
"I don't know. I mean, I don't remember telling him."
"Then he assumed you were single."

"Yes. It was a sin of omission Dulce. I have paid the price for that misdeed. He mails me the bottle and you know the rest. I'm sorry I put that perfume in your box Dulce," Vic says with regret in his voice.

"I believe you," Dulce says quietly. "Maybe you're right Vic maybe I could have come to you and ask you why you did it. Why did you do it? If you felt that way about me, why didn't you tell me in person? It was such a surprise to find an expensive bottle of perfume in my mail box."

"I should have told you how I felt in person. The indigestible problem was my being married to Lynn, who wasn't in good health. I had this longing for you I couldn't control. A part of me wanted to exorcise you from my soul. I am sure I was hypomanic at the time. I don't like talking about this.

Can we change the subject? I know. Let's talks about what happened after I left Johnson and then came back. I don't know if you can ever know how disappointed I was to find out you had left the company when I came back."

"Why don't you recap those events for us Vic. Would you like to finish off this bottle of Jack Daniels now?"

"Yes. I promise to behave like a teetotaler."

"Don't make promises you can't keep Vic," Dulce cautions as she pours what is left in the bottle into Vic's tumbler.

"Thank you," Vic says.

"No problem," Dulce replies.

Vic slowly raises his tumbler to his lips and takes a small sip.

"When I came on board at Johnson as the Supervisor of Accounting, in reality the Controller based on my job responsibilities, it was 2005."

"I'd already been working at Johnson since 1997 in Order Entry," Dulce interjects.

"Duly noted. My tenure there was initially 2005 – 2007. I am trying to remember when the perfume caper took place. It must have been 2006. I think I said that already."

"That sounds about right Victor. I think we are rehashing some of the same stuff over and over possibly because we are tipsy. It was about a year before you left the company. Why did you leave the company?"

"I'm getting to that. After you rebuked me, I decided to find another job. You weren't the only reason I left Johnson. I wasn't happy with my salary."

"You know how cheap the Johnsons are," Dulce throws in.

"That's the truth. Here I am with the fiduciary responsibilities of a Controller being compensated like a Staff Accountant. I found a job at Medical Packers in Pico Rivera and worked there in 2008. I got a ten percent salary increase."

Vic takes another sip.

"You bought my going away cake, didn't you?"

Dulce smiles.

"Guilty as charged. I figured whatever tensions there had been between us I should let bygones be bygones. How did you know I bought the cake?"

"I didn't until now," Vic grins. "When I was led into the lunch room I knew a surprise party awaited me and you brought in the cake."

"Just because I brought the cake into the lunch room doesn't mean I bought it."

"But you did buy my cake. My intuition scores another victory."

Vic displays a self-satisfied look on his face.

"I was sad leaving you behind, but I was excited about my new job at Medical Packers. I was able to partially push you out of my conscious thoughts. Things went well at first, but the company was having cash flow problems and the top management began assigning me to do things that weren't in my job description.

The bad recession that began in 2007 or 2008 really hurt Medical Packers' business. It hurt Johnson too. It hurt everybody.

It got so I was hardly doing any accounting work at all. It got so I couldn't stand to go into work at Medical Packers anymore. Finally, I reached out to Mr. Johnson to see if I could get my old job back. I returned taking a ten percent cut in pay."

"Old man Johnson hired you back at your old salary then?" Dulce asks.

"Exactly. I had no hard feelings. I was grateful to be back. If you had still been there it would have been perfect."

Vic finishes his whiskey and motions toward the waiter.

"Bring me a greyhound please."
"Yes sir."
"Bring one for this lovely lady too," Vic adds.
"What if I don't want a greyhound, Victor?"
"That's my plan. Then I get to drink it."

The waiter departs as Vic waxes philosophical.

"I was excited about returning to Johnson. The first day I went back walking up the stairs to the front lobby and I was saying to myself, 'I get to see my Dulce again'. It must have been in late 2008 or early 2009 when I returned to Johnson. The last time we saw each other was in the lunch room at my going away party in 2007. The difference between 2019 and 2007 is twelve years.

We haven't seen each other for twelve years. That's a long time for two people to be separated and apart Bravo. That's a lot of water under the bridge. Many things can change. But sometimes the more things change, the more things stay the same."

Vic pauses, stares at Dulce, who stares back. They are reliving deeply buried emotions and feeling melancholy while attempting to appear nonchalant.

"Please continue," she implores.

"Later that day after I settled in to my new old office, I looked for you in Order Entry. That's when I was told you had left the company two months earlier. Talk about ships passing in the night, eh?"

"I suppose," Dulce says softly.

"Then I was told you'd gotten married. That was the nail in the coffin. I stayed at Johnson until 2016 when I threw caution to the wind and opened my own classic car repair and restoration shop."

Their drinks arrive.

"What did you do after you left Johnson Dulce?"

"I was still at Johnson when I married Julio. He is Sophia's father. We'd been living together for years and decided to make it formal. Our parents and families were happy."

"What does Julio do for a living?" Vic asks curious about the man Dulce married and had a child with.

"He's an electrical contractor in business with a cousin of his. They always have work."

"That's a good profession. If you married him, he must be a great guy," Vic says meaning every word.

"It's not as simple as that," Dulce replies.

"What do you mean?"

"We got divorced a few years later in 2017 to be exact since we've been precise in telling each other the years things happened. I think that's the accountant part of you that's coming out. Didn't you know I was divorced?"

"I didn't know if you were still married or not."

"You agreed to meet with a married woman?" Dulce says momentarily taken aback.

Vic is thrown off balance by her question.

"No, what I meant was you would never have agreed to meet with me if you were still married. I wouldn't have agreed to meet you if I knew for sure you were married. I assumed you weren't married when you agreed to meet me. Don't forget in my email invitation I said I didn't want to upset the apple cart if you were married."

"Nice try Fontaine ten out of ten for effort."

"Why did you and Julio get divorced? Do you have a boyfriend?"

"Inquiring minds want to know, right Fontaine?"

"Are you mad at me?" Vic asks taking a long swig of his greyhound.

Dulce follows his lead and takes a long swig of her greyhound.

Dulce and Vic begin to feel the renewed effects of the liquor circulating through their bodies.

"I think we're both going to have terrible hangovers tomorrow," Dulce comments without answering his questions.

"That's why I brought Ibuprofen tablets with me," Vic says reaching into his front pocket and withdrawing two tablets.

"These are prescription strength 800 milligrams. Take one every six hours."

Dulce and Vic both take sips of their drinks.

"Please go on," Vic says with some urgency. "You were telling me you and Julio divorced in 2017."

"Yes, we did. We are still friends and he is still Sophia's dad. He is a good man like you said. Let me rewind back to 2009. After Julio and I got married I was also unhappy with my salary at Johnson just as you were. The security guard incident I told you about involving my stepmother Camila didn't help my chances for a promotion. I figured having a degree from PCC should have given me a chance at advancement. I left Johnson and hopped over to their biggest competitor Kim's Business Supplies in Santa Fe Springs."

Vic lets out a shout followed by loud clapping.

"Good for you! They didn't know what a good thing they had in you Dulce. Good for you! Street justice you jumping ship to work at Kim's. Old man Johnson was always complaining to me about Kim's Business Supplies."

Vic reaches over the table and gives Dulce another high-five.

"I'm happy for you, but if you had stayed at Johnson and still been there when I rejoined the company, we would have had the chance to start fresh."

"Start fresh? Is that the name of a toilet bowl cleaner or financial debt relief company?"

Vic guffaws at Dulce's sense of humor.

"I mean start our relationship fresh from scratch."

"You make it sound like the beginning of a tamale recipe. There was really no start fresh from scratch Victor because we had a non-relationship. Any relationship is in your head."

"Say again? If we had a non-relationship, then why are you here?"

"Forget it," she grunts.

"You know what I mean, don't you Dulce? I mean deep down inside?"

"Yeah, yeah, yeah I know what you mean," she grunts again embellishing her grunts for Vic's benefit.

He decides to switch subjects.

"Are you still working at Kim's Business Supplies?"

"I am," Dulce says radiating pride. "I am the Customer Service Manager. My degree from PCC finally paid off."

"Congratulations!" Vic says ejecting himself from his chair and giving Dulce a heartfelt and spontaneous bear hug.

"Thank you, Victor," Dulce says attempting to wrestle herself away from the head lock Vic has her in.

Their waiter, who has been keeping a close eye on the couple along with other members of the restaurant staff, all of whom have placed bets in a pool when the first real open display of romance will occur, saunters over.

"Anything going on I should know about?" he asks.

"Yes!" Vic gushes with enthusiasm. "Dulce is the Customer Service Manager at Kim's Business Supplies!"

The waiter grins and then shouts out to everybody within earshot.

"Did you hear that everyone? Dulce is the Customer Service Manager at Kim's Business Supplies!"

A round of applause echoes through the outdoor patio as Vic and the waiter gets a chant going.

"Dulce! Dulce! Dulce! Dulce! Dulce!"

After a few minutes of revelry things quiet down again as Vic releases Dulce and gives the waiter a twenty-dollar bill that he gladly accepts, a tip for services rendered.

As Vic returns to his seat he finally remembers. He begins to trip over his words almost shouting attracting more unwanted attention from everyone on the patio.

"Of course! Of Course! That it! Kim's Business Supplies is where I interviewed that time that Lynn answered the phone! Remember Dulce remember when I told you?"

"I do. You mean to tell me the job you had locked up was at Kim's the same job that Lynn messed up for you? In Santa Fe Springs?"

"Yes, Dulce, yes. Imagine that. If I had gotten that job at Kim's, which would have been in 2005, I would have worked there instead of at Johnson. If the timeline had continued as it otherwise did, you would have left Johnson and started working at Kim's in 2009.

I would have already been at Kim's in 2009 when you were hired by Kim's and maybe we could have gotten together that way. Do you comprehend Dulce? Another twist of fate that didn't fall our way. Think of it."

"I'm thinking you're overthinking Victor. Even if you had gotten the job at Kim's who knows if you would have still been there in 2009. Maybe you would have jumped ship to work at Johnson, or at another company or a job back in the aerospace industry where you used to work. Maybe in 2009 you would not have been attracted to me like you were at Johnson in 2005."

"What intrigues me," Vic muses as he begins to wax philosophic again, "Is would you have asked me if I had been in the Hitler Youth in Kim's mail room like you did in Johnson's mail room?"

"Now you are being esoteric Victor. There are many variables."
"Esoteric? Variables? Baby talk to me. When we are drunk again, which I pray will be soon, I will tell you about the Multiverse Theory."

"Drunk again? We're there Sherlock we're drunk. Multi what? Multiple verses, it that what you said?" she asks, thinking she misunderstood and wanting clarification.

"Multiverse Theory. It's engrossing. I study it as a layperson."

"Did you say it's gross?"

"Engrossing. I said it's engrossing, not gross."

"Uh huh. I can't wait," Dulce says with mock sarcasm.

Dulce has a layperson's interest in physics too, but she isn't going to let Vic know that. Not yet anyway.

She finds Vic's enthusiasm endearing. She doesn't know how long she can keep up this pretense of staged indifference toward Vic.

Dulce thinks she's been smiling too much.

# Chapter 4

## *Dinner*

"Are you ready to order yet?" their waiter asks startling both Dulce and Vic out of a mutual trance.

"What do you want Victor?"

"I don't know. Is this lunch or dinner?"

Dulce looks at the waiter. "Is this lunch or dinner?"

"Dinner," he answers smiling broadly at Dulce and Vic.

The waiter hands them dinner menus and walks away.

"This looks good," Vic gushes. "Steak and lobster enchiladas. That's for me."
"We ate that for lunch Fontaine. I mean Vic. I mean Victor," Dulce says, exploding into laughter.
"Oh yeah, we did. It was good. I'm ready for a second round."
"Sure," Dulce replies. "You are paying for this, right?"
"Oh yeah I'm paying for this baby. You're what they call on the street high maintenance," Vic answers, also bursting out laughing.

The waiter returns.

"What may I get you?"

"Two orders of steak and lobster enchiladas," Dulce replies.

"You had that for lunch," the waiter observes.

"I know. It was so good we're eating it again. It must be good because it is on the lunch and dinner menus."

"It is good. Two orders of steak and lobster enchiladas."

Vic has a dim recollection of something.

"Didn't we order pasta primavera?" Vic asks.

"Yes, you did," the waiter certifies as he collects the menus.

"Why don't I remember eating it?"

"Because you didn't eat it."

"I guess I still have to pay for it."

"I guess you still do. By the way, Happy Hour begins at 5:00 pm."

Vic checks his phone.

"It's a quarter to four now," he says. "I'll hold off on ordering any drinks until five. In the meantime, please bring us water."

Vic looks at the waiter who has been attending to them since this breakfast this morning not seeing a name tag.

"What is your name?"

"Steve," the waiter answers.

"My name is Vic. Her name is Dulce."

Vic hands Steve a twenty.

"Your water is coming right up," he says.

"Bring us both coffees please," Dulce requests.

"Now, where were we?" Vic asks.

"Right here. We've been here almost the entire day," Dulce glibly replies.

"I mean," Vic blubbers incoherently. "I mean, what were we talking about?"

"I don't think we were talking about anything Victor."

"If I call you sweetie instead of Dulce does that work for you?"

"That doesn't work for me."

Steve returns with their water and coffee.

"Thanks Steve," Vic says slipping him yet another twenty.

"Keep it," Steve insists pushing Vic's hand away. "Your steak and lobster enchiladas will be out in five minutes."

"I think I said this to you already, but you're a scholar and a gentleman," Vic stammers as Steve walks away.

Dulce reaches over and takes Vic's tumbler.

"Victor, you need to cut back. You're very drunk."
"You look very drunk yourself sweetheart," Vic slurs.
"We both need to cut back."

Dulce takes her tumbler and scoots it off to the side of their table. Then she takes the bottle of Jack Daniels and puts it on the ground by her chair.

"What did you just do?" Vic inquires.
"I didn't do anything," Dulce replies, doing her best to keep a straight face.

"Oh yes you did. Oh yes you did," Vic keeps repeating like a broken record in an accusatory tone. "I saw what you did. You absconded with my Jack. No, you jacked my Jack. Now I respectfully request that you return my Jack to its proper place on the table forthwith."

"Talk about palaver," Dulce grins, then laughing. "You can lay it on thick when you want to, can't you Victor?"
"Is palaver the same thing as malarkey maybe?" He asks.
"Malarkey maybe?" Dulce erupts into guffaws not understanding why she finds that so funny. Malarkey is such an old-fashioned word. Hours of drinking might have something to do with it along with Victor's being dangerously and delightfully delectable.

Dulce is still laughing when Steve arrives with their dinner orders.

"Steve," Vic says, "Dulce Bravo here kidnapped my bottle of Jack Daniels and now I think we need to file a police report."

Dulce reaches down, grabs the fifth of Jack and returns it to the top of the table.

"Case solved Inspector," Vic stammers to Steve, who is depositing their orders of steak and lobster enchiladas in front of them.

"This looks delicious," Dulce says smacking her lips. "I bet it'll be even better than it was for lunch."

"Bon Appetit!" Steve exclaims.

Vic reaches for the bottle of Jack Daniels as Dulce blocks his hand and moves it a couple inches toward her just out of Vic's reach.

"Victor, please eat some of your food and drink some coffee. Once you've eaten half, I will give you a shot. Deal?"

"Deal, I guess," Vic mutters in disappointment, noticing the bottle is almost empty with scarcely a shot left in the bottle.

"Are we married?" Vic asks.

Dulce begins chuckling seeing that Vic is sincere. Wasted and sincere.

"No," she replies trying not to chuckle.

"You sure do sound like a wife."

They both begin eating their food with gusto.

"You are enjoying your meal," he mentions watching her eat. "It's been my experience free food and drinks always tastes better when free. Don't forget Bravo I'm paying for these meals."

"I'm paying for it too Fontaine," she says between bites. "I'm having to put up with your company."

"When I think of you, I get highway hypnosis," he says.

"Sounds like a personal problem."

Vic tells Dulce a secret.

"Off the record I'm not as smart as I look," he shares with her in confidence.

"Off the record you're not as dumb as you sound," she swiftly replies.

⁂

"That was the best meal I have ever had in my life," Vic concludes as he leans back after putting away his steak and lobster enchiladas.

"You mean the second-best meal," Dulce observes as she is eating Vic's Caesar Salad that comes with that meal after having finished hers. "That's what you said when you ate those same steak and lobster enchiladas for lunch."

"May I drink now?" He asks.
"You may. You have a full stomach now," she says.
"Thank you."

He lifts his glass to his mouth and swallows some of his greyhound.

"Why don't you tell me about yourself Bravo. What do you do? A day in the life."
"I already told you I'm the Customer Service Manager at Kim's Business Supplies. In fact, I already told you the story of my life. Are you having a senior moment Fontaine?"
"I'm not a senior according to AARP and the government."
"Do you want me to recap my entire life Fontaine? Or recap our relationship, such as it is. My bad. We don't have a relationship."

Steve takes away their empty plates thinking about the bet he placed on the time these two will finally seal the deal on a public display of their affections.

Vic decides to try another angle and poses a question.

"Would you like me to tell you about the Multiverse Theory?"
"What?"
"The Multiverse Theory."
"What is that?"

"I thought you'd never ask," Vic responds while winking at Dulce.

Vic takes a conservative sip as Dulce is searching Google for Multiverse Theory on her phone. He then picks up his own phone and searches for Multiverse Theory.

Dulce sees Vic scrolling his phone.

"What are you doing?"
"Looking for the Wikipedia article on Multiverse."
"Way ahead of you Fontaine. I have it. I thought you were going to tell me about it. Why are you are having to look it up on your phone like me? If you are an expert on the subject why don't you just tell me?"
"I'm not a physicist Bravo," he hisses.
"Neither am I. That is why I searched for it on my phone."

Both of them read the beginning of the Wikipedia article on Multiverse.

"Good grief Victor," she says. "This stuff is complicated."
"It is Dulce."

Vic has a question.

"Doesn't your name mean sweet in Spanish?"
"Yes," Dulce says distracted.
"You are well-named," he comments dryly openly leering at her.

"What do you think about the theory?" he asks quickly changing subjects trying to reign in his libido.
"I'm still reading about it."
"How about if I read the summary out loud?"
"If it pleases you Fontaine please do."
"There you go again alternating between calling me Victor and Fontaine and sometimes Vic."
"You've been calling me Bravo Fontaine."

Vic begins reading from the Wikipedia online article on Multiverse.

"The multiverse is a hypothetical group of multiple universes. Together, these universes comprise everything that exists: the entirety of space, time, matter, energy, information, and the physical laws and constants that describe them. The different universes within the multiverse are called 'parallel universes', 'other universes', or 'alternate universes'."

"If you are trying to bore me to death mission accomplished. May I ask you a question Vic?"

"Always."

"What has this got to do with anything?"

"Good question. Forget all the what appears to be gobbledygook. I have spent dozens of hours thinking about this. I know I am not a scientist, but after great mental effort on my part I believe I finally penetrated the veil of understanding of the Multiverse."

"Veil of Understanding? Is that the name of a book I should be familiar with? Did you mean to say you finally read the Veil of Understanding? Or did you mean The Veal of Understanding that award winning cookbook showcasing the best of bovine husbandry?"

"Aren't you funny," he says smirking then giggling. She is sharp as a tack, he thinks, feeling aroused on multiple levels while discussing multiple universes.

"That was funny," she says in agreement.

"Let me cut to the chase Dulce. The Multiverse Theory says anything that can happen does happen in alternative universes to our own. In different alternate realities."

"And your point is?" she queries.

"Well, take the day of the perfume caper where I put the Dulce Bravo perfume in your mail slot at Johnson. According to the alternate universe theory there is another reality where you didn't go to Human Resources, but instead you came to me."

"Alright then, according to the alternate universe theory there is another reality where you didn't put the perfume in my mail slot at all, but rather you came to me and told me how you felt."

"That is true too," Vic agrees. "Remember when we were talking about what if Lynn hadn't booby-trapped my chances to work at Kim's? Same thing. Sorry to repeat myself, I think I just said that a few minutes ago I'm not sure, but if I didn't listen to me. If I did, listen to me again. I'm having an attack of stream of consciousness."

"Stream of what? Stream of consciousness? Is that your favorite fishing hole?" she jokingly asks.

"No. It means. Hmm. I forget what it means. Never mind. I'm digressing."

"Yes, you have a digressing problem," she diagnoses. "You should have a doctor check that out during your next checkup."

Vic decides he can't win this battle and goes back to his stream of consciousness, whatever that is.

"In an alternate universe I would have been working at Kim's instead of at Johnson if Lynn hadn't messed things up and we would have met in 2009 when you went to work at Kim's instead of 2005 when I went to work at Johnson leading us into new variables. Remember you used the word variables? You understand what I mean."

"You are thinking too much and you keep going over this if only scenario with Kim's and repeating yourself Fontaine. This is metaphysical."

"Metaphysical?" Vic says incredulous that she would know that word. "How long did you wait to spring that word on me?"

"Don't you know what metaphysical means Victor?"

"You bet I do," he says trying to search for the meaning of metaphysical on his phone on the down low.

"No cheating Fontaine. I see what you are trying to pull. You don't know what it means do you? Tell me. Tell me what metaphysical means."

"I used to know what it means. Sitting here at this moment I can't recall what it means. Can you tell me what it means?"

"It is a branch of philosophy concerned with existence and the nature of things."

Vic is baffled, confused and very impressed. And very aroused.

"How did you know that off the top of your head?"

"I took a semester of philosophy."

After the first protracted period of silence they've had since they began chatting at ten this morning Vic speaks up abruptly changing the subject.

"What is your favorite movie?"

"I have several movies I like," Dulce states.

"Do you remember 'A Few Good Men'?"

"That's with Tom Cruise. I believe it also starred Jack Nicholson and Demi Moore."

Vic scrolls on his phone.

"It is amazing that almost everything is on the internet. I found some of the dialogue between the characters in that movie. You remember the 'You can't handle the truth' scene, don't you Dulce?"

"I think so. It was at the end of the movie."

"It is when the Tom Cruise character had the Jack Nicholson character on the witness stand. You want to have some fun?" Vic asks.

"More fun than we've had up to now?"

"Totally more fun. We've had fun today and now we are going to have even more fun!" Vic says with some forced bravado.

"Doing what?" Dulce asks skeptically.

"Playing the characters in movie scenes using actor dialogues I found online!"

Vic hands his smart phone to Dulce.

"Find that website that's on my screen and we can go back and forth together."

"This is your idea of having even more fun?"
"Yes. It'll be more fun."

Dulce begins to chortle.

"Maybe it would be fun. Maybe. Okay, let me find the website. I'll use your keywords."

Dulce quickly finds the website and hands Vic's phone back to him.

"Why don't you go to the dialogue in the scene between Galloway and Kaffee that starts off with 'But my feeling is'. You play Galloway the female Navy Lieutenant and I will play Kaffee the male Navy Lieutenant."

"But Kaffee only has one line," Dulce objects, noticing what the line says.

"It'll be a dry run for us," Vic says smoothly, trying to suppress a smile as he takes a sip of his greyhound.

"Are you ready?" Vic says just a tad too eagerly.
"Ready as I'll ever be. I think I need to take a sip of my greyhound too."

Dulce sips, clears her throat and then begins reading the text for Galloway from her phone.

*"But my feeling is that if this case is handled in the same fast-food, slick-ass ' Persian Bazaar manner with which you seem to handle everything else, something's gonna get missed. And I wouldn't be doing my job if I allowed Dawson and Downey to spend any more time in prison than absolutely necessary, because their attorney had pre-determined the path of least resistance."*

Vic reads the short text for Kaffee with flair.

*"Wow. I'm sexually aroused, Commander."*

Vic can't hold it in any longer and begins laughing so hard he begins to gag. Dulce joins him in the hilarity as Steve comes over.

"Are you guys alright?" he asks with some concern.

"We're fine Steve," Vic manages to get out in between heaving chuckles. "We were just having some fun."

"I see," Steve says, grinning. "I thought somebody was choking."

"We may have been choking on our lines," Dulce manages to say, breaking down in tears as Vic reaches over and gives Dulce a third high-five.

Steve walks off seeing that all is well, or all seems to be well, with the two lovebirds. The restaurant crew has been rotating watches keeping a constant eye on the blooming romance at the corner patio table.

Dulce and Vic smile at each other.

Then they both finish their greyhounds as Vic scrolls down looking for some more lines from 'A Few Good Men'.

"Here's one," Vic blurts out with vigor. "It's the one that starts out with Galloway saying, 'I'm sorry, I should have called first'. See it?"

"I found it. I guess I am Galloway again. You want me to begin now?"
"Go for it. I'll follow your lead."

"Why am I always the one who goes first?" Dulce murmurs as she clears her throat again. Then they begin reading the lines.

> *Galloway: I'm sorry, I should have called first.*
> *Kaffee: No, I was just watching a ball game. Come on in.*
> *Galloway: I was just wondering if you'd mind me taking you to dinner tonight.*
> *Kaffee: Are you asking me out on a date?*
> *Galloway: No...*
> *Kaffee: It sounded like you were asking me out on a date.*
> *Galloway: No, I was just...*
> *Kaffee: I've been asked out on dates before, and that's what it sounded like.*
> *Galloway: Do you like seafood? I know a good seafood place.*

Dulce begins giggling. "Did you hear what I said, or rather what my character said? Seafood! I'm allergic to seafood."

"It was nice to hear you asking me out on a date," Vic says with his own giggles.

"Did you hear what Galloway said Victor? She said no to that question," Dulce clarifies.

"If you say so. It just sounded like you were asking me out on a date," Vic says attempting to mimic the Tom Cruise Lt. Kaffee character.

"Let's see what else can we do," Vic states. "Oh, here it is. The famous 'You can't handle the truth' scene. Are you finding it?"

Dulce nods her head yes.

"How about I be Jessep and you be Kaffee?"

"Sure," Dulce says accepting her assignment.

"If you watched the movie you saw the emotion that Jack Nicholson and Tom Cruise put in the lines. Let's put our hearts into our lines Bravo. It's only five lines. Are you ready?"

"Victor, you're first up as Jessep."

> *Jessep: You want answers?*
> *Kaffee: I think I'm entitled.*
> *Jessep: You want answers?*
> *Kaffee: I want the truth.*
> *Jessep: I love you!*

Vic turns beet red and looks up at the sky as several patrons crane their necks after hearing him practically scream out, "I love you!" which echoed and reverberated throughout the outdoor patio and into the indoor dining area.

Dulce is staring at Vic with an enigmatic smile. He notices an uncanny light in her eyes.

"You fumbled the last line, Vic," she says cool as a cucumber. "You were supposed to say, 'You can't handle the truth'! Despite fumbling the line, you really put your heart into it."

Steve is spreading the word among the restaurant staff that Vic told Dulce 'I love you'. Sensing that his presence might be needed Steve walks over to their table post haste.

"You guys need anything?"
"I could use a drink," Vic say without hesitation.
"I figured you might," Steve replies, then lowering his voice, says, "I'll bring you out a greyhound on the house."
"You have no idea how badly I need a greyhound Steve."

Steve looks at Dulce who indicates she doesn't need another drink.

Dulce clears her throat to break the uneasy quiet.

"Would you like to redo those last five lines again Victor?" she asks doing her best not to smile. That was beyond cute, she thinks to herself. That was beyond adorable. That was just beyond.

"No! No, that's fine. I think we've done enough line reading for now."
"It was fun," Dulce says in her most bubbly voice.

Steve returns with Vic's greyhound, which he grabs and guzzles half-way.

Dulce wants to continue saying movie lines.

"Vic, I also liked that other military themed movie called 'An Officer and a Gentleman'. You're familiar with that movie, aren't you?"

Vic takes a long swig draining his greyhound.

"I remember that movie. It had Richard Gere and Debra Winger in it."
"That's right Vic. Very good. You must be a movie buff. I found some quotes from that movie on the same website. It has quotes from all kinds of movies. You wanna do some more lines?"

Vic feels the greyhound taking away his angst at his massive Freudian Slip. He is also vaguely aware that if he had a nickel for all the times he's told Dulce he loves her in the email barrage he sent her via Marisol he would have a dollar.

It's not like she doesn't already know he is in love with her.

"I found the lines for the scene where Mayo and Paula are in the hotel room," she says coyly. "You remember that scene?"

"I think so," he says uncomfortably.

"Why don't you go to the 'An Officer and a Gentleman' link. You'll see the lines. This website has everything well organized."

"Okay," Vic says reluctantly, wondering what his next faux pas will be.

"You will play Mayo and I will play Paula. Are you ready? You are first up again."

> Mayo: What do you want? You want to fuck? Is that what you want? You wanna fuck? All right, come here. Get on the bed. Take your clothes off. I'll give you a good fuck.
> Paula: Where's that coming from?
> Mayo: Get on the bed.
> Paula: I wouldn't fuck you now if my life --
> Mayo: Then get the hell out of here, because I don't need this shit.
> Paula: I don't know who you think you're talking to, you know. I'm not some whore you brought in here. I'm trying to be nice to you. I'm trying to be your friend, Zack.
> Mayo: Well, then be a friend. Get out of here.
> Paula: Fine. Fine. You know, man. You ain't nothing special. You got no manners. You treat women like whores. And if you ask me, you ain't got no chance of being no officer.

Vic begins chuckling.

"Something funny Victor?" Dulce says trying to suppress a grin.

"Was that last line of yours of Paula speaking supposed to send me a message?"

"No more than your flub of Jessup's last line earlier," she responds suppressing a smile.

Vic smiles at Dulce thinking, 'I got a Jones for that woman'.

"Are we doing anymore lines from 'An Officer and a Gentleman'?" he asks.

"I think that's enough movie talk for one day," she replies now smiling at him warmly.

Dulce shares a last thought.

"'An Officer and a Gentleman' has a happy ending."

# Chapter 5

## *Closing Time*

Stave walks over as Dulce sees several men bringing in large speakers and other musical equipment.

"What is going on?" Dulce asks Steve pointing at the men.
"Music starts at five. Tonight, the DJ will be playing a lot of mambo music. You can dance."
"I took mambo dance lessons," Vic slips in looking at Dulce.
"If you think I am going to dance with you Fontaine think again."

Vic is gazing steadily at Dulce.

"Oh, you're gonna Tango with me alright Bravo."
"You sure about that?" Dulce asks challengingly.
"I am," Vic says.

Dulce giggles under her breath.

"Why would you take mambo lessons?" she asks.
"Because," he replies.
"Because what?"
"Just because."
"I don't think you took mambo lessons," she flatly states with certitude.
"They were rumba lessons actually," he confesses.
"Then why did you lie to me?"

"I fibbed. I didn't lie."

"Sounded like a lie to me."

"You are splitting hairs," he says in mild annoyance.

"You're just mad because I called you out on your deceit."

"Deceit? Deceit?" Vic repeats getting worked up.

Vic waves at Steve.

"What can I get you?"

"Steve," Vic says, "Is it a lie to say you took mambo lessons when you really took rumba lessons?"

"Well," Steve contemplates, treading lightly, not wanting to interrupt the flow of twenties that have been coming his way all day, "It is inaccurate. However," he quickly adds, "They are both dance lessons."

"Thank you, Steve," Vic says, eyeballing Dulce as he transfers a twenty-dollar bill to Steve, who takes it this time.

"I rest my case," Vic says to Dulce.

Dulce sees through the thin veneer of his façade and finds it irresistible.

Steve points at the men and equipment.

"Looks like they are about ready to begin. It is almost Happy Hour. Would you like a greyhound Vic?"

"Yes Steve," Vic replies. "And this time bring the lady a glass of your finest red wine. It's for the anti-oxidants, right Dulce?"

Dulce finds it interesting he remembers her making that comment.

"Red wine will be fine," she attests. "I'll drink it even though I probably shouldn't be mixing red wine with greyhounds."

"Coming right up," Steve says as a man begins to speak over a speaker.

"Good evening ladies and gentlemen. I am The Big Bopper your DJ host and I hope everyone is having a wonderful time on this lovely Friday night in scenic Laguna Beach.

Tonight, we are going old school and will start off with some classic mambo music. For those of you who may not know what that is I am sure once I begin playing mambo songs you will recognize it.

If any of you want to dance, or try to dance, to the music please indulge yourselves. This is a lively tune recorded by Perez Prado called 'El Manisero', which means 'The Peanut Vendor' in English. Although this is mostly a mambo night this song is considered responsible for launching the rumba dance craze in the USA back in the day."

Steve returns with their drinks. They both take long sips as music starts to play.

"I like that song," Vic says to Dulce. "It has a nice steady beat to it."

"Come on, dance with me," he pleads, standing up and extending his hand towards hers.

"I may regret this, but why not," Dulce says taking Vic's hand as they go out to the dance floor.

The song fills the patio as Dulce and Vic and two other couples meet on the dance floor. They begin talking over the music standing in the middle of the dance floor face to face.

"Okay Fontaine, the DJ said this is a rumba song. Let's see you do those rumba steps you took dance lessons for."

"Can we make a deal Bravo?"

"I'm listening."

"Let's improvise, like in jazz."

"Sounds like you're trying to weasel out of something Fontaine. Lucky for you I'm in a good mood."

"I'd hate to be with you when you're in a bad mood."

Dulce and Vic begin dancing around improvising getting in sync smiling at each other as the steady beat of the song 'El Manisero' makes it easy to swing and sway at a measured pace. The song ends as everyone claps and The Big Bopper comes on the microphone once more.

"You are looking good tonight my peeps! To those of you still in your chairs we have plenty of space for more couples on the floor. This next tune is a real mambo song. This one was also recorded by Perez Prado. It's called 'Qué Rico Mambo', which means what a great mambo song. And it is. It is sometimes called 'Mambo Jambo' in English. Put on your dancing shoes because here it comes."

The song begins at a fast pace as Vic takes the led and motions for Dulce to twirl around as he lifts her right hand over her head. Dulce laughs and they repeat the process this time with Vic twirling around. The second stanza of the song slows up and they continue their improvisation.

Then the song picks up the same pace again in the third stanza of the song and as Dulce is twirling Vic, he loses his balance and whirls into a table that luckily is unoccupied because the couple who had been sitting there is dancing.

Vic crashes into the table sending two half-eaten meals on two expensive plates and two expensive wine glasses filled with vintage wine flying as he manages to grab the table to keep from hitting the floor face first.

The Big Bopper cuts the song off as Dulce rushes over to him. She manages to help Vic stand up. Guacamole is dripping from his sports coat and pants and is beginning to drizzle down from the top of his head. Parts of Maine Lobster are splattered all over him. It's a mess.

"Are you okay?" Dulce asks as Steve, The Big Bopper, the couple who had been sitting at the targeted table and several lookie loos rush over as Vic steadies himself on his feet. Dulce guides him back to their table as Steve and the restaurant manager are assessing things.

Vic eases into his chair feeling like he is going to be sore in various parts of his upper and lower body come morning where he flew across the table.

Dulce is making an extraordinary effort not to laugh as guacamole oozes down the right side of Vic's face from the top of his head. She figures he must have made a direct hit on the guacamole. He takes several napkins and begins to wipe off his face as Steve makes an appearance. That didn't take long. Vic has a feeling Steve is the bearer of bad news.

"What's the damage?" he inquires before Steve can open his mouth.

"I have an itemized total, most of which were the two meals they were eating and the appetizers, replacement meals we are preparing for them including appetizers, along with the bottle of vintage wine they were drinking and the replacement bottle of vintage wine they will be drinking. The two broken expensive wine glasses and two broken expensive plates are unsalvageable."

"How much?" Vic asks in exasperation at the whole situation.

"$476.34 including tax and excluding gratuity," Steve replies, sympathy resonating in his voice.

"I told the manager you and Dulce have been here since breakfast. The tip is on me since I also served that table. I have an itemized list of the damages if you'd like to see them."

"I trust you," Vic says reaching for his wallet. He feels a sharp pain in his right hand as he lifts his wallet out of his pants pocket. He figures he must have hurt his hand when he tried to break himself as he was careening across the table. His right thigh is beginning to throb. This misadventure aggravated the muscle pull in his lower back he got this morning climbing up the stairs to the gazebo.

Vic gives Steve five C-Notes and tells him to keep the change.

"How much is my tab for our meals and drinks so far? I assume you have been keeping track."

"The preliminary total including tax is $313.56."

"But not gratuity," Vic assumes.

"Correct. You have already been generous in that department so consider it waived. I slipped in those freebies like the French Toast and several drinks."

"You are an officer and a gentleman Steve. I mean a scholar and a gentleman. No worries my man I can cover my tab."

Dulce has been desperately stifling an urgent need to laugh and can no longer contain its release. She explodes into an avalanche of belly laughs.

Vic sits glumly bummed at what happened as she continues with nonstop laughter that is coming in waves. Dulce is laughing so hard she is starting to feel weak like she is going to pass out.

"I'm sorry sweetie," Dulce lets slip out instantly realizing her mistake. Vic perks up. He thinks, did she just say what I think she just said?
"What did you say?"
"I'm sorry Vickie. I called you Vickie and I meant to say Victor. You know I'm drunk."
"No, no, no," Vic admonishes moving his right index finger back and forth at her.
"I heard what you said. You said, 'I'm sorry sweetie'. I'll wager you ten bucks that's what you said."
"You can think what you like Fontaine and I don't gamble," she replies, slipping into laughter again as Vic joins her in the merriment his pain notwithstanding.

Steve, standing at the outside register, can hear the animated high spirits coming from Dulce's and Vic's table and begins to laugh himself. No doubt about it, he thinks, they are in love. That is also the consensus of the rest of the restaurant staff including the manager.

Steve knows there is something familiar about Vic, but he can't put his finger on it.

The song 'Qué Rico Mambo' starts up again and the dancing resumes.
"Shall we dance?" Dulce asks, erupting into more laughter as Vic joins her.

"No way. I couldn't take any more guacamole," Vic comments. "I've had enough for one day. You know, it tastes pretty good."

They both double over in a laughing jag.

"I should take my Ibuprofen now," he says taking a tablet out of his inside sport coat pocket. "I'm surprised my two tablets weren't damaged during my mishap."

"No!" Dulce exclaims uncompromisingly. She feels a protective maternal instinct kicking in. "Don't take any prescription med with alcohol especially with the amount you've consumed today."

"You're right. Thank you, Dulce," he says sincerely returning the tablet to his pocket. "Maybe you are my Guardian Angel."

Dulce smiles inside at his comment trying not to let it show in her face.

"Why did you agree to meet with me?" Vic asks catching Dulce off guard, but she recovers nicely.
"To make sure you are not a danger to society and to yourself."
"Coming from my Guardian Angel I will take you at your word."

Dulce decides to turn the tables.

"You got us a hotel room, didn't you?" she boldly asks.
"How did you know?" he asks a look of surprise written all over his face.
"A little birdie told me," she curtly replies trying to maintain her deportment and look serious.
"Did this little birdie have your name on it?" he asks, figuring she must have tailed him.
Dulce decides to take it a step further.

"Are you trying to hit on me?" she asks aggressively.
"I'm trying to make a love connection, but I won't say that," Steve answers not able to contain a half moon grin expanding on his face.
"That's what I thought," Dulce responds flashing a grin as wide as Vic's.

Dulce and Vic begin moving back and forth to the nonstop music being thoughtfully provided by The Big Bopper while staring down each other.

Vic signals Steve.

"It's getting to be late afternoon. Before the sun begins to set and it gets dark please take some photos of Dulce and me. I am incompetent at taking selfies."

"Hey! Who says I want to be in a photo with you?" Dulce says pretending to be annoyed.

"I do baby," Vic replies.

Vic gives his phone to Steve and he lifts his chair, wincing at the pain in his right hand, and puts his chair down next to Dulce.

Steve moves forward trying to get the best camera angle. "Good thing this is an iPhone," Steve says. "I know exactly how to use it."

"Cool," Vic says, scooting his chair right up next to Dulce's.

"Lean in to me," he says, coaxing her.

Steve has found a good camera angle.

"Ready? Say cheese!"

Vic adroitly puts his arm around Dulce just before Steve pushes the white Photo button.

Steve shifts his position and takes several more photos of the pair and returns Vic's iPhone.

"That's what I'm talking about," Vic says in appreciation to Steve. "There will be a little something extra in your paycheck this week."

Vic checks out the photos and shows Dulce, who merely bobs her head privately happy the photos were taken.

"These are great," Vic exclaims moving his chair a few inches closer to Dulce.

"Get back to your spot," she says.

"My spot? Who says we have spots? What if I don't want return to my spot?"

"I might have to call Security and have you forcibly moved back to across the table from me."

"You think you can intimate me? Huh? Is that what you think?"

"That's what I think."

"You know what Bravo?"

"What?"

"You scare the hell out of me. I'm going back to my safe space."

Vic slowly stands up wincing from pain in his right thigh, lifts up his chair only with his left hand, and goes back to his original spot directly across from Dulce.

Dulce sees that Vic is in some distress.

"Are you okay?"

"I think so," he replies. "I hurt my right thigh and my right hand when I had my accident."

"You have my permission to take one of your Ibuprofen tablets if you don't drink anymore tonight."

"Forget it," he responds. "Booze will be my Ibuprofen until before I go to bed when I will take one."

"Where will this bed be?" she asks giving him a sly smile.

"No comment," Vic says getting turned on by her flirtations.

"Can I make a true confession?" Vic requests.

"Do I look like a priest?" Dulce says evenly trying to maintain her composure.

"It really turns me on to have your permission."

"I have a dog collar with a long chain you can wear around your neck," she says in a silky voice feeling aroused remembering her other comment to Vic about a dog collar.

"I was hoping you would wear the one I have," he counters.

"I hope handcuffs come with the dog collar and chain," she says.

They stare at each other.

The plot thickens.

"I have another true confession," Vic says.

"Then I definitely need a drink," Dulce says as she takes a long sip of her red wine.

"Sometimes I dream about you."

"You told me that already. You like repeating yourself."

"I was testing to see if you were paying attention," Vic manages to say, finding crossing brains with Dulce exhausting and exhilarating.

Vic keeps hearing Dulce's phone pinging and ringing with incoming text messages and calls from her brother Joaquin. This has been going on all day. Vic almost mentions it, but lets it go.

Dulce wonders when she should discuss Vic's drug money laundering trial with him. It needs to be discussed. It must be discussed. If anything is going to happen between them, if they are ever going to have a relationship, she must know. Dulce wants to get inside Vic's head on the topic of his trial and acquittal.

"I'd like to revisit our discussion on intuition," Vic says after an extended pause. Vic thinks if he keeps up the pressure on Dulce she will relent and succumb to his charms eventually. He thinks he is well on his way to fulfilling that goal.

"Intuition? We go from handcuffs to intuition?" Dulce says smirking.

"We're versatile people capable of conversation on many levels," Vic replies with aplomb.

"Okay Fontaine, you want to chat about intuition again? Chat."

"You admit I was correct about 'The Sound of Music'?"

"We've already gone over this."

"You admit it, right?" Vic says prodding.

"Yes, I admit it. What more do you want?"

"I wanted to hear you say it one more time."

"Okay so you heard it. Anything else?"

"Yeah. I want to know if you declared bankruptcy when you and I both worked at Johnson at the same time."

"What? What are talking about?" Dulce is caught off guard by his query.

"Bankruptcy. Did you, or did you not, declare bankruptcy?"

"No. Yes." Dulce admits. "It wasn't me it was my stepmom."

"I knew it!" Vic says in a loud voice.

"What's your point Fontaine?"

"My point is my intuition told me so."

"That type of information is available in public records and like I said it wasn't me who declared bankruptcy."

They both take sips of their drinks.

"It was medical bankruptcy," Dulce continues. "I worked with the attorney. Her medical bills were so high even though her insurance paid for most of it."

"Same thing happened to me at that same time," Vic candidly tells her. "In my case, it was from unpaid bills from my late wife Lynn from many hospitalizations over many years. I just knew it was happening with you too in some capacity, at some level."

Dulce and Vic stare at each other.

"Anything else?" Dulce asks.
"Two last things. Two last intuition related questions for you."
"I'm listening."
"You are religious and you catch colds easily."

Dulce slowly smiles.

"Now that's lame Fontaine."
"True or not true Bravo?"

Dulce squirms uncomfortably in her chair.

"True or not true Bravo?" Vic asks again raising his voice.

"True," she admits.

Vic breaks out into a wide grin.

"I'm four for four Dulce," Vic states with conviction.

"More like one for four," Dulce replies in pretend annoyance. "I will concede 'The Sound of Music' and only 'The Sound of Music'. The others were lucky guesses or contrived."

"Good enough," Vic says continuing to grin, feeling like he has the upper hand. "'The Sound of Music' is all that really matters."

Vic feels like he has mojo.

"I'm batting a thousand and I going to get to third base if not home plate before the night is over. I can see the coach waving me in to home like what happened to you."

"You'll be lucky if they don't throw you out at first. Make that if I don't throw you out at first."

Dulce takes a sip of red wine and decides to drop a hint.

"Do you want to know what's counterintuitive Fontaine? You being on trial for laundering drug money. You struck me as a nerd at Johnson despite the perfume incident or perfume caper as you call it. Seeing you on the witness stand being cross-examined for laundering drug money in a big deal trial was surreal."

If that doesn't get him to talk about the drug trial nothing will. She changes the subject.

"You still have guacamole on your face Victor," she says.

Vic ignores her observation.

"I'd like to visit imprinting," he says.

"Imprinting? Is this a business you own?"

"No," Vic says adroitly, trying not to let on how cute and sexy the look on her face is.

"Imprinting is a theory I have about what was going on with you and me at the time I began working at Johnson Industrial Supply."

"Oh brother," she says, as she drains the rest of her red wine noticing he has a cute dimple.

"I'm not your brother I'm your lover," Vic responds his greyhound running interference for him.

"In your dreams Fontaine," Dulce fires back.

"That's right Dulce dear I do dream about you."

Dulce decides on a strategic retreat seeing that Vic is in the zone.

"I'm waiting," she says. "Imprinting. You said were going to tell me about imprinting. While you are talking, I am going to check online to see if you are full of soup, as opposed to being full of something else."

Vic drains the rest of his greyhound and flags down Steve for another round for him and Dulce.

"You see Ms. Bravo, when I first encountered you in the mail room, my intuition was at a high level. You remember me telling you about Eric Berne?"

"Yes, I recall Mr. Fontaine."

"I didn't tell you specifically about Eric Berne's experiment."

"Is this going to bore me?"

"Why no, not at all. As I was saying Ms. Bravo right after the end of World War Two Dr. Eric Berne was helping to out process soldiers from the Army. He discovered when he was tired, he was able to guess with a high degree of accuracy the occupations the soldiers had held in civilian life."

"What does this have to do with the price of beer in East Los Angeles?"

"Nothing. But it does have something to do with You and I."

"I'm not connecting the dots. Would you make your point?"

Vic loses his concentration as Steve brings them their greyhound and red wine.

"What was I just talking about Dulce my dear?"

"You were babbling some nonsense about an experiment by Eric Berne and soldiers."

"Yes. Now I am not sure what point I was trying to make."

"You also babbled something about imprinting."

"Imprinting! That's it. See, my intuition told me those things about you like how you like the movie 'The Sound of Music' the same way Eric's intuition told him about the civilian occupations of the soldiers. This is what happened in the mail room when you asked me if I was in the Hitler Youth."

"I still say you might have been a member," Dulce answers breaking into subdued chuckles.

"I'll ignore that darling. The bottom line is my theory says you imprinted on me."

As Vic was talking Dulce had been doing some online searches.

"Fontaine, now I know you are full of soup and I am being polite. Listen to what this says about your so-called theory of imprinting:

'Imprinting, psychological: A remarkable phenomenon that occurs in animals, and theoretically in humans, in the first hours of life. The newborn creature bonds to the type of animals it meets at birth and begins to pattern its behavior after them. In humans, this is often called bonding, and it usually refers to the relationship between the newborn and its parents'.

Imprinting is when baby ducks are born and see their mother for the first time. Are you saying you saw me and like a baby duck decided to follow me?"

Vic stares at Dulce finding her more than enchanting.

"That is not what I am saying at all Bravo. You are misconstruing my meaning."

"Meaning? You can't even define what you are trying to tell me."

"I told you already 2004 and 2005 were two of the worst years of my life. No, Lynn's death and the drug trial in 2018 were worse. It was a one-two punch. First Lynn dies, then a few months later I was arrested for laundering drug money. I digress again. Because of what happened to me in 2004 and 2005 I was impressionable. You impressed me. You still impress me."

"I thought I imprinted on you."

"Imprinted, impressed now you are playing word games. Maybe you imprinted on me and impressed me."

"I think you are the one playing games. Didn't your buddy Eric Berne write a book called 'Games People Play'?"

"How did you know that?" he asks, astounded that she would not only have knowledge about that book, but that she would also be able to roll that book off her tongue impromptu.

"There's lots you don't know about me," she blithely replies.

Vic, seeing that Dulce is winning this round, backs off.

"Anything else you want to talk about?" she asks him grinning like a Cheshire cat.

"As a matter of fact, there is," he replies. "Care to guess what it is?"
"Your trial?"
"How did you know? You have good intuition."

Dulce straightens up in her chair and gets serious despite her chronic inebriation.

"You will talk to me about it?"
"Naturally. Couples shouldn't have any secrets between them," Vic says solemnly.

Dulce sidesteps a snappy comeback to Vic's couples' comment as he stands up and drags his chair over next to her and sits down.

"What are you doing Fontaine still trying to get me to call Security and have you forcibly removed to your side of the table?"

"No Bravo if I am going to give you the skinny on my goings on with my trial I am going to have to whisper in your ear."

"As long as they aren't sweet nothings."

"They aren't sweet and they aren't nothing," he retorts without rancor.

They both take long sips emptying their glasses. Steve meanders over and upon seeing they have finished their drinks without asking he declares, "Drinks coming right up."

They listen to the music The Big Bopper is playing as Steve brings them their replenishment alcohol.

"It's getting dark," Vic observes, taking a sip.

"Yes, it is. Do you have any more astute observations to make Mr. Science?"

"I have a serious question to ask you Dulce no kidding."

Dulce sees this is important to Vic.

"I'm listening," she says with barely concealed affection for him that she fears is ready to spin out of control at a moment's notice.

Vic motions for Dulce to lean her head down slightly into his as their noses almost touch. Steve deposits their drinks grinning at the two of them huddling together wondering when the cuddling together will begin.

"Hand on Bible tell me you are not an undercover cop or an FBI agent with a wire," he whispers.

"Hand on Bible I am not an undercover cop or an FBI agent with a wire," she whispers back relishing the moment and the sensations traveling up and down her spine.

Vic moves close to Dulce their shoulders touching. He detects the freshly washed shampoo smell of her long thick black hair. More than a hint of perfume begins a welcome intrusion into his senses. He feels her right knee slightly tapping his left knee.

"You don't drive a Ford Crown Victoria Police Interceptor or a Police Interceptor Utility Vehicle then?"

"No, I don't Victor. I drive a Honda," she says, briefing touching his forearm with reflexive affection that takes her by surprise.

"You don't how happy that makes me," he says, taking a deep sniff of her perfume that makes him feel lightheaded.

"I'm happy you trust me," Dulce says emotionally flipping her hair back.

"I would trust you with my life," Vic categorically states their noses almost touching.

Dulce crosses her left leg towards Vic, her high heel caressing his ankle and calf.

"Your right leg still hurt?" Dulce coos at him in his ear like a dove.

"Only a little. Your shoe massage eases the pain."

"Happy to be of service."

"I need a drink bad," Vic says as his heart rate jumps. As Vic reaches for his greyhound with his right hand, he slides his left arm around Dulce's upper body. Dulce shifts right in her chair and pushes her body into Vic, then extends her right arm around Vic's waist.

Dulce leans her head on Vic's shoulder as he gulps down the rest of his greyhound and waves at Steve, who yells out, "Coming right up!"

Steve and the rest of the restaurant staff have been keeping tabs on the unfolding romantic drama at the corner table and start giving each other knuckle bumps.

One of the cooks begins collecting on his first-place winnings from the betting pool that had been set up a couple hours earlier involving the entire crew. The runner ups including Steve also collect on their winnings.

Steve delivers the greyhound for Vic and another glass of red wine for Dulce.

"Where were we?" Vic asks rhetorically as he takes a healthy swig of his latest greyhound.

"You were going to tell me about your criminal past," Dulce replies.

After looking around casing the joint especially the immediate outdoor patio area she whispers a note of caution in his ear, "Don't forget to whisper. That is important to remember."

"The darkness and the music will act as a cover as long as we whisper and we are lucky to be in a corner location on the patio," he says. "I only have a last request to you before I tell you about my criminal past. It can be summed up in four letters. DBAA."

"DBAA? What does that mean?"
"It means 'Don't Be An Asshole'. I learned that from the TV drama series 'Breaking Bad'."

Dulce and Vic begin laughing as their foreheads gently collide.

"OMG I'm LMAO because of DBAA," Dulce says coughing because she is laughing so hard.

Thankfully the greyhound has its intended effect, allowing Vic to be able to focus somewhat on regaling Dulce with his drug money laundering adventure and keep at bay the intoxicating aroma of her thick luscious hair and sensually stimulating perfume.

Vic starts whispering as he squeezes her waist with his arm and begins rotating his hand and fingers on her back as she snuggles up even closer.

"It was the most traumatic period of my life that was both a curse and ultimately a financial blessing in disguise. Even though I beat the rap I was guilty of being an accessory after the fact. When I realized what was going on, I went along. I was legitimately afraid for my life. I was also greedy."

"I want to understand you," Dulce states unequivocally.

"Are we addicted to each other?" Vic asks.

"Addicted to love maybe," she replies.

"Are we in love?" he innocently asks in his fog.

"Maybe addicted to love like I said," she responds not wanting to go there directly just yet.

"'Addicted to Love' was a rock song by Robert Palmer. How did we get started on this line of questioning?" he asks.

"I don't know."

"Are we still drunk?" he asks.

"Very," she confirms.

"That's what I thought."

Dulce rubs her head against Vic's shoulder as Vic squeezes her.

"Where were you?" she

"Ah, not sure. Where did I leave off? Now I remember. I'll try to pick up where I left off. That's funny. Pick up where I left off."

"What's funny about that?" Dulce asks snickering.

"I have no idea."

"Then get back to your story."

They giggle. Then Vic picks up where he left off whispering.

"Without that what do you call it watershed event in my life 'Vic's Classic Car Restorations' would have died on the vine before it became successful. I wouldn't be living the good life in Laguna Niguel either in a beautiful condominium. I used to be the kind of guy who lived on the installment plan wallowing in self-pity. I owe my success to dirty drug money Dulce."

Dulce processes this information happy that Vic has regrets, but despite herself part of her inner self finds it compellingly attractive that he was involved in the netherworld of Cartel drug dealing and drug dealers. He and his partners in crime were on the news for weeks on end. She thinks Vic doesn't look like a bad boy. He most likely doesn't have tattoos. Neither does she.

One thing she knows for certain. It feels good to have his arm wrapped around her.

"Before you get too deep into the drug Cartel, tell me how you started your car business," Dulce whispers in Vic's ear, her lips touching his lower left ear lobe. "My dad owned a garage and restored old cars. He restored a '57 Chevy Bel Air."

Vic is dumbfounded and pleased as punch as this revelation. Now he has something in common with Dulce's dad. Then he remembers Dulce said her dad is dead.

"You said your dad died?"
"Yes, of a heart attack. My two brothers took over the shop. They still have the '57 Chevy. It was restored to the original specifications."

Vic stirs in his chair.

"Really! That's something. Do you have any idea how much an originally restored 1957 Chevrolet Bel Air is worth? Is it two-door or four-door?"
"Two-door."
"Convertible?" he eagerly asks.
"You know it is."

Vic violates the whisper rule and hollers out, "Unbelievable!"

He returns to whisper mode whispering in her right ear.
"I think your brother Joaquin and I can be buddies. What's your other brother's name again?"
"Gustavo. He's the brother of mine who runs the shop day to day."

Vic lifts his tumbler as Dulce lifts her glass. Vic speaks as low as he can.

"I propose a toast. To your family's garage, to your dad, to your brother Gustavo and last but not least to your brother Joaquin. Joaquin might not be the most sociable fellow in my regards, but he'll come around to liking me."

"He still thinks you're a nut case. He's been texting me all day warning me what a dangerous person you might be. You're not a dangerous felon are you Victor?"

"Not as dangerous as you," he replies, as they begin to laugh for the umpteenth time.

You want to know who I really am sweetheart?"

"Who are you Victor Fontaine?"

"I'm your Knight in Shining Armor who'll take you to his castle as we ride off into the sunset."

"I like that," she responds.

"Let's get back to your car business. Tell me all about how it got started and how you became such a dangerous criminal."

Vic nuzzles his nose into her hair enjoying the scent of her hair and perfume.

"Is that Dulce Bravo perfume you're wearing?"

"If I said yes would you believe me?"

"I believe anything you tell me," he says kissing Dulce's forehead waiting for the right time to kiss her lips.

"Back to my car business. I had scrimped and saved and with a loan from the bank I took the plunge. It was a huge gamble, but I wanted to pursue my dream of owning my own business and over the years I've developed some friends because of my Camaro. What was, uh, what is the word oh yes what was fortuitous is the loan officer at the bank was an acquaintance I'd met at several classic car shows and that was a big help because he authorized the maximum loan amount. I was nervous, but anything like that is a risk and a gamble."

"I've heard my brothers talk about that," Dulce says.

"About what?"

"About overhead and cash flow and the costs in starting and maintain a business even though my father already had our business going by the time he passed away and they took it over. I remember my father being worried sometimes when business got slow. I know it's tough to start a business is what I'm saying."

"You said our business. Are you a partner?" Vic asks, his interest peaked.

"Yes, in my father's, that is, in my papa's will he left me one quarter stake in the shop, so I have an ongoing interest in keeping up with what is happening with it."

"What's the name of your shop?"

"'Bravo's Car Repairs and Restorations'."

"I suppose in a way you compete against me. But I mostly service Orange County and you guys have East L.A., The South Bay and West L.A. I have several clients in West L.A."

"There's enough business for both of us," Dulce says, snuggling.

"We could always do a merger," Vic says, squeezing Dulce.

"How is 'Vic's Classic Car Restorations' doing these days?"

"Business couldn't be better. I have pangs of guilt about that."

"Is this because of the trial and all that you were involved in before that?"

"Yes. It's a long story."

"I've got time."

"I need a potty break," Vic says.

"Me too. Meet you back here."

As Steve watches Dulce and Vic rise from their table and walk by him holding hands and wobbling a little heading for the restrooms, he'd already observed they'd started speaking to each other in a very low voice. He assumes the lovers are whispering sweet nothings in each other's ears.

As Dulce and Vic enter the main dining area a few cheers break out along with scattered clapping. On this night and in this restaurant, they have become minor celebrities with the customers and the staff.

Vic follows Dulce into the ladies' room, who begins to howl. With tears flowing from an overdose of laughter she guides him out by the hand and leads him to the men's room.

They return a few minutes later to their table resuming their exact positions taking generous sips of their drinks.

Vic continues talking and Dulce continues listening. The alcohol steadies Vic and enables him to tell his story without negative flashbacks.

"I was telling you how I got my business started with a generous loan from my bank because of my insider connection with the loan manager of my bank branch. It's true what they say about golf."

"What do you mean it's true what they say about golf?"

"I formed a business and personal relationship with this guy on the golf course. That paved the way for me to get a business loan from his bank on favorable terms."

"I see what you mean. Go on Vic. Stop interrupting yourself and tell your story."

"Inquiring minds want to know?"

"Something like that."

Vic regains his train of thought.

"Where was I? Oh yes. I was worried my medical bankruptcy was still on my credit report. I wasn't sure if it was or not and I didn't want to know that's illogical but it is what it is. Ignorance is bliss inertia. I was concerned they knew about it.

Even with favorable loan terms it didn't take long for me to get in over my head. In my zeal I hadn't fully considered all of the expenses."

"But you're an accountant Vic. A Controller. I remember the Johnson family thought highly of you."

"I know, but I messed up anyway. Business was good right from the start. I got that part right my market research was spot on perfect. The problem was I was only breaking even. The biggest problem was I had was turning business away because I couldn't handle the throughput. That was the extra business I needed to start turning a profit. I let my emotional desire to open up a classic car restoration shop override my common sense."

Vic turns his head to the left and puts his chin on the top of Dulce's head.

"That wasn't the only time I let an emotional desire override my common sense."

"I'm glad you did," Dulce says, squeezing Vic's waist. "You needed to expand the size of your garage, right?"

"Right, at a minimum by five bays because that is what I needed to have in order to turn that elusive profit I was telling you about. I didn't have the capital I needed to expand. My bank had done all they could and I wasn't going to be winning the lottery, or Publisher's Clearing House, or have a rich old uncle die and leave me with a surprise inheritance. It was so frustrating Dulce to say no to new business because I didn't have the garage space and I couldn't afford the expert body shop people I needed."

"Good body shop workers are hard to find for specialty restoration. When did you start your business?"

"In April, 2016 I resigned from Johnson and opened up shop. My garage was located in Redondo Beach at the time and I was living there too. It was a reasonable lease the best I could find. I did two things right before I opened. I got the market research right and I got a good lease. You could even argue I got great terms on my bank loan. But everything else went downhill fast. When you are starting a new business, it doesn't take much to tip the scales towards the negative."

"That's only three years ago. You went from rags to riches?" she wonders.

"Something like that. A few months after I opened the garage a man driving a Royals-Royce Phantom pulls in. He was well-dressed and spoke English well, although I could tell English wasn't his native language."

"Spanish was," Dulce surmises.

"Yes. He told me his boss had a 1960 Aston Martin he wanted restored. I told the man I was booked up and he opens his wallet and thrusts $20,000 at me. I was initially disbelieving and then tempted, but the next restoration opening wouldn't be for two weeks. I told him this and I added how sorry I was because I needed the work, but I told him I was barely making ends meet.

Two days later just after I'd opened the shop the same man stops by driving the 1960 Aston Martin his boss wanted restored. He comes in and hands me some paperwork and says he'll leave the Aston Martin at the address on the enclosed paperwork, which I immediately read, which turned out to be a new lease. My old lease was cancelled.

I don't know what magic was used, but before I had a chance to say anything the man quickly walked away. I was intimidated thinking something isn't kosher about this. I felt like I was watching something on Netflix instead of it happening in real life. I thought maybe this is a blackmail attempt or extortion. I was scared.

I drove to the address in Laguna Niguel and to my surprise a couple mechanics were already working on the Aston Martin. The same man was there and gave me an envelope. He told me to read what was inside and quickly did an exit stage left.

The only thing listed on the enclosed sheet of paper inside the envelope was a toll-free number. I was almost ready to call the authorities when I decided why not call the number. In retrospect I realized they no doubt had me under surveillance already and would have known if I called the FBI or police."

"What did you do? You called, correct?" Dulce says, rubbing her head into Vic's shoulder.

"Correct. It was a pre-recorded message saying a mystery man has dozens of cars needing to be restored and I didn't have to worry about anything. All I had to do was sit in my office and pretend I was running things. I knew something was wrong with that picture, but I told you about my cash flow situation and no doubt they knew about it too. That's how it got started."

"You were scared."

"Scared and terrified."

"Anyone would be. You must have figured you were dealing with some high roller criminals."

"That's what I figured. They figured me right that I would do what they said. Far as I knew my phones were bugged, my office was bugged and I saw listening devices everywhere. I was paranoid."

Having noticed Vic's voice was beginning to get a little louder Dulce says, "Don't forget to whisper."

"Thanks. Keep reminding me."

"How does this tie into your drug money laundering trial?"

"I'll get to that. I began receiving shoe boxes with hundred-dollar bills in them every morning I came into the office. Each shoe box had $5,000 in currency in them always C-Notes always neatly organized in thousand-dollar wraps. Then one morning I arrived and inside the shoe box was an envelope with a set of keys and real estate paperwork for a condominium with a Laguna Niguel address."

"Let me interrupt you and summarize. You were receiving $5,000 every day in cash in shoe boxes and now you own a swanky condo. Did you put your money in a bank?"

"I called that number again and this time instead of a prerecorded message I got a human who asked me what I wanted. I explained to him I wanted to put the money into a bank, or some of it and how can I do that? I had been receiving these shoe boxes for five months."

"You never asked what it was all about?"

"No. I knew it was probably related to an illegal drug operation. These guys weren't gang bangers staking out a few blocks of turf downtown. I determined it had to be savvy drug dealers. Big players."

"Cartel types," she comments. "That's who it turned out to be. It all came out in the trial. I followed it closely."

"Yes. I didn't know that until the trial, but it wasn't a surprise. I didn't want to know who I was dealing with. My mindset was 'I know nothing'. Back to my phone call. I was told somebody would contact me. To make a long story short the next day I received a visit from a guy who looked like a member of the Kiwanis Club and owned a successful upscale restaurant. What I mean by that is you wouldn't peg him as having anything to do with the Cartel."

"You can't judge a book by its cover," Dulce notes.

"True. This guy had set up several bank accounts in my name and the equivalent amount of the shoe box money was deposited into it without any scrutiny. I had three accounts one of which was a phantom yet real account. It was extremely sophisticated. I never took the CPA exam, but I'm telling you no CPA I know or ever knew could have pulled that off. It was off the grid and off the charts."

"Wait a minute Vic. How much money had accumulated and where did you keep it? You just went to this bank and stood in line at the teller with a shopping cart full of shoe boxes with five grand each in them and then said to the teller I want to deposit whatever amount it was into this bank account?"

"No. The equivalent amount of the money in the shoe boxes was deposited and I had to return the money contained in the shoe boxes. I'd been keeping the shoe boxes in the basement of my new condo under a canvas. The Cartel knew exactly how much money they had given me as hush money. As far as the amount of money that was deposited are you ready for this?"

"I can't wait," she says, feeling stimulated by their conversation.

"Are you ready?"
"I'm braced."
"$750,000 and change."

Dulce jumps in her chair momentarily tightening her grip on Vic.

"You okay?"
"I'm fine. You did say $750,000 and change."

"I did. And that was for starters. That was only five months' worth of salary or payoff money or bribery money or hush money or whatever it was. This went on for two years before I was arrested."

"I suppose you want to know the grand total to date?"
"Come on you know I do," she pleads.
"$3,600,000 and that is a low-ball number."
"Oh," she stutters in stunned disbelief.

Dulce removes her arm from Vic's waist and sits up straight in her chair trying to grasp and process this unfathomable information.

Steve notices a break in their tête-à-tête and walks over.

"You guys need anything?"
"A drink," Dulce loudly shouts.
"Red wine?" Steve asks.
"Yes, and a double-greyhound for Vic."
"Change in my order Steve. Bring me two glasses of red wine," Dulce says.
"Coming right up."

Dulce and Vic begin holding each other again as Vic begins speaking in his normal tone as Dulce quickly cuts him off.

"Whisper!" she loudly whispers to him.

"Thanks. Now you want to know how I was able to beat the rap."

"I do. It sounded like for most of the trial the prosecution had you dead to rights."

"One would think. I thought they did too."

"Why aren't you in San Quentin Prison or Folsom Prison instead of sitting here with me?"

"All I can come up with is it must have had to do with some sophisticated accounting and financial sleight of hand. If you remember nobody from the Cartel actually went to jail."

"That's true. Turned out to be much ado about nothing and wasted taxpayer's money from what was reported after the trial," Dulce comments in awe, completely transfixed.

"It was about something for sure," he continues. "I never knew how they were able to launder money through my classic car restoration business. My speculation is they bought older cars and knowing there is a legitimate market for older cars that are classics especially here in SoCal they fronted their drug money through the car transactions. I was restoring over 20 cars a day and business is still good. Nowadays it's all a legitimate business."

Dulce sees Steve striding toward their table with their drinks and scratches Vic's back as a head's up, who stops whispering.

"Thanks Steve," Vic says handing off another twenty to Steve.

Vic resumes his saga this time remembering to keep whispering.

"Were the employees legitimate? Do they still work for you?"

"They do. It's don't ask don't tell. I don't ask them and they don't ask me and I don't tell them and they don't tell me. You could say it is like the acronym MAD between the nuclear powers meaning Mutually Assured Destruction. They've all been checked out by the feds and as far as the feds are concerned 'Vic's Classic Car Restorations' is as clean as a whistle."

"It's still incredible to me you were able to get off the hook."

"You mean beat the rap. Well baby, I beat it. I beat the rap. The prosecution couldn't prove their case beyond a reasonable doubt. I have to give the Cartel attorneys a lot of credit. They managed to obfuscate as they say legally and by a manipulation of the clueless in the news media and above all the twelve jurors. I have a lot more to tell, but can we continue this discussion at another time? It dredges up bad memories for me."

"What did it feel like to be found innocent and released from jail?"

"It was a swing of emotions from the depths of despair to the heights of happiness."

"Stated like a poet Vic. Just one more question. Make that two more questions.

First, is the $3,600,000 you told me about is still unaccounted for? Who knows about it?

Second, how did you feel when you were arrested? How did it feel being incarcerated in Men's Central Jail during your trial? Why didn't you post bail? How did the feds even suspect you in the first place?"

"Sounds like more than two questions. Here are my answers. Only you and me know about the $3,600,000. Make that three if we include the clean-cut Cartel accountant, but we don't have to worry about him. I don't know how this money was and remains undetected, but I am able to access the funds and use them. There is more to the story, but let that suffice for now. They didn't post bail for me because that might have been a red flag for the feds.

Life at Men's Central during the trial was tough, but I had respect among the cons because of the nature of the trial. I got into an argument one time with a screw, that's prison jargon for a guard, on the question of whether or not an unoccupied cell needs to be locked. It was funny. This screw and I argued the point for a half-hour before I convinced him it didn't need to be locked."

"Promise to tell me the rest later?" she begs. "I want to know more about your arrest. About Genome Genetics that was a big part of the trial. There is so much more I want to know about."

"Promise," he promises.

"I'll tell you a true confession Vic."
"I'm waiting with bells on baby."

"I've been hiding the truth from you much of the day about my feelings. I worried about you during the trial. I thought about you. I thought about how you were doing and about your well-being."

"Thank you for telling me that means a lot," he says. "Dulce, when I was in lockup, I discovered the less I felt, the more I could stand the emotional and psychological strain. The not knowing was the worst part, the uncertainty of what was coming next. There were many long nights when I thought I would be spending the rest of my life in San Quentin Prison or Folsom Prison."

Vic caresses Dulce's back.

"During those long nights in lockup at Men's Central after a long day in court, or hours spent strategizing with my Cartel lawyer, I thought of you. I knew whether or not I spent the rest of my life in prison I was already serving a life sentence as a prisoner of love. I was destined to be a lifer for you Dulce. I want to serve my full sentence."

Dulce caresses Vic's back.

"I never understood how and why you evoked such strong feelings in me Vic. How and why you could push my buttons so easily. It was as if you could reach inside me and caress my soul as you are caressing my back now. There was a vacant place I had within my heart that nobody had ever been able to penetrate until now. Over these last twelve years I thought about you a lot. I am so happy you reached out to me."

They both take healthy sips of their drinks as Steve comes over to their table.

"Closing time in ten minutes folks," he says.

Vic looks at his phone.

"Nine fifty already!" he exclaims in astonishment jettisoning the ballast of those bad jail cell and drug trial memories stat.

"Time flies when you're having fun," Steve says grinning at Dulce and Vic.

"It sure does," Dulce replies, hugging Vic.

"Shall I bring you the bill?"

"I really wish you wouldn't do that Steve," Vic says erupting in guffaws. "Yes, bring the bill. We're about ready to leave."

Just as Steve is ready to walk over to the outside register, he turns on his heels.

"That's it! Now I know who you are! Vic Fontaine! Vic Fontaine from the drug trial!"

"Okay, okay calm down. It's true I am Vic Fontaine. I was proven innocent. You want my autograph anyway?"

Steve chuckles.

"I won't bother you with that, Vic. I know how celebrities hate it when people ask for their autographs. I want to thank the both of you for giving us a great show today of true love in action. We had a pool with everyone betting on when you two would publicly exhibit your affections. One of the cooks won $200.00 for first place. I won $50.00 for third place."

"On top of all the tips I gave you," Vic says good-naturedly. "Just bring me the bill."

"Sure thing Mr. Fontaine."

"Sounds like you have a fan club. I could start a Vic Fontaine fan club. Steve and I can be charter members," Dulce says, laughing while spilling a splash of her red wine on the table.

"Careful darling," Vic says. "Don't get any wine on that lovely dress. Red wine would be hard to get out."

They drain the rest of their drinks gulping them like they were drinking water instead of booze.

Steve returns with the bill. Vic sees the grand total is $376.56 excluding gratuity. Without any prodding Steve says, "Don't worry about the gratuity."

"I wasn't," Vic says deadpan like a comedian with perfect timing.

Steve withdraws four C-Notes from his wallet and tells Steve to keep the change. Vic is feeling very tipsy once more.

Dulce takes off her high heels and puts on her flats and puts her heels in her oversized purse where the flats were. She came prepared for all contingencies including bringing binoculars.

Before her rendezvous with Vic, Dulce had a premonition and intuitive feeling Eric Berne notwithstanding that today would be an interesting day.

"You ready to go honey?" Vic asks.

"Yes sweetie. Where are we going?"

"Out into the rhythm of the night to the gazebo, where our day began."

"Sounds dreamy," she replies and they get up and stagger step over some bushes almost tripping making it to the walking path heading to the gazebo.

Steve and the staff are applauding and cheering Dulce and Vic from the patio as they walk off into the darkness waving goodbye to the restaurant staff.

The staff begins a raucous chant, "Dulce and Vic! Dulce and Vic! Dulce and Vic!"

They hold hands unsteadily negotiating the pedestrian path overlooking the ocean as the chanting and cheering fades into the night.

A full moon is hanging in the sky.

# Chapter 6

## C'est Si Bon

Dulce notices Vic is limping slightly favoring his left leg as they walk along the path bathed in moonlight toward the gazebo.

"Does your right leg still hurt?"

"My right thigh and my right hand hurt from my crashing into the table. My lower back also hurts. I hurt my back this morning climbing up the stairs to the gazebo. I must have pulled or wrenched a muscle. Crashing into the table made it worse. I'm a walking commercial for pain creams and pain medication."

"I'll slow down so you can keep up with me," she says.
"Thanks. I don't think I've ever had that much to drink."
"Me neither. We drank too much. I'm grateful neither of us threw up. With the amount we drank it was a distinct possibility."
"We calibrated our drinking responsibly and did most of our drinking during our meals. Don't forget Dulce Bravo we drank over the entire day."
"That's my point Victor Fontaine we drank over the entire day. We did a lot of drinking on empty or semi-empty stomachs."
"Look, sweetheart, we know how to hold our liquor otherwise we would have spilled out cookies already."
"You realize we are still drunk," she cautions.
"Do I ever," he replies chuckling.

The gazebo looms in sight.

"It looks pretty in the moonlight Vic. Come on," she says, beginning to drag Vic with her.
"Slow down," he says.
"Oh sorry. We're almost there."

They enter the gazebo and walk to the wooden railing overlooking the ocean.

"It so beautiful Vic," she says.
"It is," he replies looking at her.
"See how the moonlight highlights the waves?"
"The waves look like they're dancing."

Vic is scrolling unsteadily on his phone finally finding what he was looking for.

"Whatcha doin'? she slurs.
"Looking for a song that has reminded me of you and me for years."
"Really? What song?"
"It's called 'Spartacus Love Theme'. I heard it on an FM station a few years back. I found out it was written by orchestral composer Alex North. Listen to it."

Vic plays a YouTube version on low and they listen.

"It is haunting and beautiful and reminded me of you," he says as the song ends.
"I like it," she remarks. "I remember hearing it from the movie 'Spartacus'. It does have a haunting quality. A sad melancholy quality."

The look at the ocean for a minute. Dulce puts her arm in Vic's arm as they lean over looking at the ocean view.

"I anoint you Suavecito, Dulce Bravo," he says.
"What did you say sweetie?"

"I said Suavecito. That's your nickname now. Suavecito. It's the name of a song I heard on the oldies station once."

"It means 'soft' and 'softly'. It can also mean 'cuddly' and 'soft little one'."

"I know. It fits you."

"That's sweet. I'll have to find a nickname for you."

"You have already. Sherlock. You've called me Sherlock a couple times."

"Sherlock it is. Suavecito and Sherlock are our official nicknames."

"Is it me, or are the stars spinning?"

"It's not you," Dulce says. "The stars are spinning. We drank way too much today. I know I did. I feel queasy."

"Ditto on the queasy," he acknowledges.

"The red wine and greyhounds and Jack Daniels must be hitting us in waves," she speculates. "I know another relatable song that might not be as haunting as the 'Spartacus Love Theme', but it is just as meaningful," she says teasingly.

"What song is that?" he asks.

"Try to guess."

"'Something Good' from 'The Sound of Music'," he intuits.

"You're right! You're right!" she starts shouting her voice echoing off the beach rocks below.

Dulce quickly grabs her phone and forces herself to find a link. She takes Vic's phone out of his left pants pocket and succeeds in finding the same song link in spite of being drunk.

"Are you a pocket pick? I mean are you a pick pocket?" he garbles. "What are you doing with my phone?"

"Finding that song you mentioned."

"What song?" he asks not remembering what he said.

"'Something Good'," she blurts out.

"I said that?"

"Yes, you did, silly. Your brilliant intuition at work again. The link is set on your phone. Let's watch it together."

They hold each other as Dulce holds up her phone. Dulce and Vic watch the love scene between Maria and The Captain that ends with their singing the song 'Something Good'.

As it ends Dulce says, "I love the words 'Nothing comes from nothing, nothing ever could'."

"So somewhere in my youth or childhood, I must have done something good," Vic chimes in.

He could never have planned the unplanned chorus only a spontaneous ad hoc approach could have worked. Spontaneous, ad hoc and enormous amounts of booze, that is.

They put their phones down and hug each other tightly.

"'Now let's sing 'I am sixteen going on seventeen' from 'The Sound of Music'," he states matter of fact.

"How did you know that? How? How did you know I was thinking about that song? You did it again! I don't believe it you did it again!" she starts shouting at the top of her voice, actually screaming and piercing the night's silence.

"It was elementary, my dear Watson," Vic says laughing. "After all, I'm Sherlock Holmes and you're Dr. Watson."

Vic is vaguely aware he is doing something good, but he is not sure what it is, but whatever it is it is making Dulce very happy. He remembers hearing her say something like nothing comes from nothing, so he must be doing something good because whatever he's doing can't come from nothing.

Dulce quickly grabs her phone and forces herself to find a link. She grabs Vic's phone out of his hand. He doesn't notice.

"Whatcha doin'? he slurs trying to keep the gazebo roof from moving in a clockwise direction. Or is it moving in a counter-clockwise direction?

"Finding that song you mentioned."

"Song? What song?" he asks once again still not remembering what he said in his alcoholic haze.

"'I am sixteen going on seventeen' from 'The Sound of Music'," she says.

"I said that?"

"Yes, you said that Sherlock. I want us to dance the way Liesl von Trapp and Rolf Gruber danced. We're in a gazebo like they were. I have link for the web address set on your phone same as mine. Here's your phone back. Let's watch it together."

Dulce plays the song outtake from the movie with Liesl and Rolf.

"You think you can dance to that?" she asks.

"In here? The gazebo is turning round and round in circles," he protests mildly.

"Sure, why not dance in here. Liesl and Rolf did. It's so amazing you guessed the song Vic. I can't believe it. Please dance with me. You're not drunk you said we can hold our liquor. You wanna watch the video again?"

"Nope, I got it down. Are we going to sing too?"

"Yes. Let's do this. Let's both start the video at the same time with the speakers on loud and we can follow what they are doing. Can you handle that big boy?"

"Ain't nothing to it."

"Are you ready? They talk at first and begin singing pretty fast so pay attention."

"Ain't nothing to it Suavecito. Or should I call you Liesl?"

"Call me Liesl and I'll call you Rolf!" she enthuses walking on clouds at this extraordinary turn of events.

"Get ready to play the link I've set Rolf. Don't drop your phone."

"Same for you Liesl."

Dulce places Vic face to face in front of her in the middle of the gazebo.

"Play!" she orders.

Vic has a momentary false start, but begins to get with the program as his phone begins broadcasting the song 'I am sixteen going on seventeen' as he does a karaoke like imitation following the male actor's lead who is playing Rolf.

Dulce does the same thing following the female actress who is playing Liesl.

They are bouncing around running into each other laughing themselves to distraction as they both try to keep up not only with the singing, but the dance movements of Liesl and Rolf on the video they are taking peeks at as they twirl and swirl around inside the gazebo.

Vic feels his right thigh throbbing and his lower back aching, but sucks it up because Dulce is having such a good time dancing and singing.

"Good thing there isn't any guacamole around this time," Vic says in between the lyrics.

Dulce begins bellowing out laughs and almost falls backwards.

Vic is almost ready to collapse, but notices in the video that Rolf is now approaching Liesl apparently to kiss her. Just as he is about ready to emulate Rolf and reach out and kiss Dulce, an unwelcome intruder spoils the festivities.

"What do you two think you're doing?" a man in a police uniform calls out from the path.

They halt aware they are no longer alone. An unwelcome intruder has made his presence known. Dulce turns off the music on her phone and does the same for Vic's phone.

Vic suddenly feels like he is going to vomit. Despite that uncomfortable feeling, he takes the initiative.

"Officer, Liesl and I were rehearsing lines for a school play we are going to be in Friday night."

"School play?" the officer asks skeptically. "This is Friday night."

"I meant Saturday night. Yes sir, Saturday night."

"What school?"

"High school."

"You're too old to be in high school."

The officer walks into the gazebo.

"I received a complaint about two people causing a public disturbance. You two are lit up, gassed up and drunk as skunks."

"I take exception to your tone and false accusations, officer. I can assure you sir we are not lit up," Vic utters defiantly. "We might be drunk as skunks, but we're not lit up."

Dulce is leaning into Vic trying her best not to laugh and trying ignore the moving walls of the gazebo.

"There's one way to find out," the officer says. "I'm going to conduct a field sobriety test on the both of you."

Dulce takes the initiative.

"Officer, aren't field sobriety tests only used for those suspected of driving under the influence?"

Vic takes the opportunity to put his foot in his mouth.

"Yeah officer, are you going to arrest us for dancing under the influence? I admit that's a DUI."

He breaks down laughing as Dulce tries to hush him up.

"Go stand over there," the officer orders, pointing to a corner.

Dulce takes Vic by the hand and pulls him with her to the corner as the cop ordered.

The cop keeps a wary eye on them as he bends down, takes a piece of chalk from his pocket and begins chalking out a white line on the floor.

The officer begins chalking and talking.

"I have a probable cause for arrest. Two individuals publicly drunk making loud noises and causing a public disturbance."

Despite Dulce's best efforts she can't stop Vic from inane commentary.

"We were dancing to 'The Sound of Music' officer. It was my big chance to score with my girlfriend."

The officer finishes drawing his chalk line and stands up.

"What's your name?" he demands looking straight at Vic.

"Rolf. I'm a telegraph delivery boy. I'm in the SA."

"In the what?"

"SA. According to research I did to impress my girlfriend Liesl SA means Sturmabteilung in German."

The officer's patience, already wearing thin, begins to melt away.

"Get over here Rolf. I want to see some ID. You stay there miss."

"She's a near miss officer," Vic stammers, giggling. "Get it? Near miss? She's divorced and – "

"SHUT UP!" the officer yells at Vic.

"Listen to me carefully Rolf. Put your left foot on the line, then place your right foot on the line ahead of your left, with the heel of your right foot against the toe of your left foot.

Do not start until I tell you to do so. Do you understand?"

Vic stays quiet.

"Do you understand?" the officer says aggressively.

"I understand," Vic finally says.

"Walk that line," the officer barks at Vic.

"Do you still want my identification sir?" Vic asks meekly his wallet halfway out of his pocket wincing in pain. "You see sir, I hurt my right hand today office because I ran into a tree. No, I ran into a table. What did I run into today Liesl baby?" Vic asks glancing over at Dulce.

Dulce is desperately trying to keep a grip on reality not sure if she is Liesl or Dulce. She decides she is Dulce and needs to ameliorate the situation.

"You see officer," she begins in as steady a voice as she can muster, "We were on a date – "

"Then you do admit it was a date and not a meeting!" Vic screams out in joy.

"Both of you keep quiet," the cop snarls. "Walk the line!"

"Isn't that the name of a Johnny Cash song?" Vic says unsuccessfully trying to put one foot in front of another along the chalk line.

"It's called 'I Walk the Line', the officer corrects. "That song has good memories for me."

"Then I'll sing it for you," Vic volunteers. "I hear it once in a while on the oldies station I listen to," as he teeters off course almost falling down.

Vic launches into an off-key rendition of 'I Walk the Line' as the officer begins to laugh.

He walks over to the officer and says to him, "Let's get with the program."

Soon they are both singing the song 'I Walk the Line'.

"You need to keep your day job Rolf," the cop says offering some free and friendly advice.

The officer returns to officious mode and orders Vic to return to Dulce's side.

"Are you two planning to drive?" he asks.

"No sir, we're planning to have a tryst at the hotel," Vic says. "I'm going to try to have a tryst with my new girlfriend Liesl. That's my plan. It's going to be what you call a team effort."

"Where is this hotel?" the cop asks, trying to keep a serious facade and not show his growing amusement.

No answer is forthcoming from Vic because he can't remember. Dulce comes to the rescue.

"The hotel is down the hill officer on PCH. It's within walking distance just around the corner."

Vic turns to Dulce, "You did follow me Liesl!"

"I did," she responds, doubling over laughing, as does Vic.

"You knew all along since lunch I was planning for us to have a hotel tryst."

"Ten-four good buddy," Dulce says.

The officer looks them over.

"I'm going to let you off with a warning this time. You must promise me not to drive. Do you promise?"

"I promise," Dulce says. Then turning to Vic, she says, "Say it Rolf, tell the officer you promise."

Dulce punches him in the ribs. "I promise," he says after being her punching bag.

"Remember, no driving. Go to the hotel now. Good night," the cop says walking away humming, 'I Walk the Line'.

"You're an officer and a gentleman," Vic hollers out. "You're a gentleman and a squalor too," he adds.

"You said squalor," she says. "It's scholar for Pete's sake. You said the same thing to Steve."

"I mean scholar," Vic corrects, hollering out his correction and once again disturbing the silent tranquility of the Laguna Beach night.

"Let's get out of here," Dulce says with a sense of urgency alarmed that they aren't out of the woods yet.

"I can't wait to get to the hotel too," Vic says believing that is the urgency to which she is referring. "We're on the same page baby doll. Let's get to that hotel room pronto."

"We've got to walk down those stairs Rolf, I mean Vic," she says trying to keep on an even keel.

"If I don't accept the mission to walk down the stairs the secretary will disavow any knowledge of my actions, right Liesl?"

"What are you talking about? I'm Dulce, Vic and not Liesl. We were, uh, we were having fun."

"Are you sure you're Dulce Vic and not Liesl?"

"Yes. It's Dulce Bravo not Dulce Vic. I'm not Liesl and you're not Rolf. We were playacting don't you remember?" she says, surveying the immediate area for pedestrians and police.

"If we were married your name would be Dulce Vic," he states incorrectly.

"If we were married my name would be Dulce Fontaine."

"Wouldn't you be hyphenated?" he asks.

"If we were married my name would be Dulce Bravo-Fontaine."

"What is Rolf's last name? Oh, now this is important Liesl. When I was talking about not accepting the mission, I was referring to that old retro TV show Mission Impossible. Ever watch it?"

"NO!" she yells becoming concerned that same cop might make a return trip and might not be so understanding the second time around.

"Listen to me Vic because you're drunker than me. We're going to walk to the top of the stairs. When we get there, I want you to hold to the rail with your left hand and hold on to me with your right arm. Can you do that?"

"I'm going to puke," Vic replies, quickly limping off the path just making it to a bush. He sounds like he's losing a lung. Dulce scans the area afraid someone else will call the police.

"Are you alright?" she asks as Vic slowly stands up from behind a bush.

"You don't know how good it feels to feel good," he says.

"You seemed like you were feeling good before you vomited," she says.

"How are you feeling?" he asks

"I feel a little nauseous myself. I think I can make it to the hotel. Come on, we got to get out of here. If we don't that cop will be back and put us in the drunk tank."

Dulce believes a repeat of her briefing instructions to Vic is in order.

"This is important Victor listen to me carefully. We're walking to the top of the stairs. When we get to the top of the stairs you must hold on to the rail with your left hand. You will walk down the stairs on my left side. You will put your right arm around me and hold on tight. Can you do that?"

"That sounds like a possible mission I can accept Dulce dear not a mission impossible. Do you want me to put my right arm around you now?"

"No, let's save that when we go down the stairs. The stairs aren't far away. Come on, hold my right hand with your left hand," she beseeches.

"Why not have me hold your left hand with my right hand?"

"You hurt your right hand and right leg dancing. I'm trying to find a way to minimize your pain."

"Now that you mention it, my right hand and leg do hurt. So does my lower back. I have prescription strength Ibuprofen I can take."

"You can take it later. Hold my hand. We must get out of here!" she says insistently.

They slowly walk together reaching the top of the stairs. Dulce looks down at the steep stairs below that are moving back and forth and thinks here they are both messed up, Vic is hobbling and what could possibly go wrong? She positions Vic to her left.

"Place your left hand on the railing. Do it."
Vic complies.
"Put your right arm around me."
Vic complies.
"Start with your right foot. We'll step down together. Let's try it."
They take their first step.

Vic remembers an oldies song he likes.

"There's a song called 'Step by Step' by the 'Crests'. Here we are at the steps. Shall I sing it for you? I've listened to it so much I know the step lyrics."

"NO! Don't sing it," she demands. "Stay quiet! You want that cop to return and bust us and put us in jail?"

"Well, that cop likes Johnny Cash. I can sing a Cash song. I could sing for cash. What's it worth to you if I sing 'Step by Step'?"

Dulce prods Vic to take a second step as Vic breaks into song.

"Step one, we had a date; and then we stayed out late and I walked you home."

"Vic, listen to me. You must focus on keeping your balance. If you sing, you might fall."

"I'm falling for you Liesl," Vic says loosening his grip on the railing.

"LOOK OUT!" Dulce screams as Vic slips and slides down a stair dragging her down with him.

"That was close," he says, recovering. Dulce helps him up grateful he doesn't have a sprained or broken ankle. That's all we would need, she thinks.

"Keep holding the rail and stick out your foot when I do and we'll get to the bottom. You must cooperate with me. You must be careful. I'm serious. You must take this seriously."

"Are we playing footsies?"

"Yes, Vic we're playing footsies. Come on, follow my lead."

Vic cooperates as they steadily make their way down the steps and finally reach the bottom practically unscathed.

They walk toward the sidewalk along PCH. Vic is limping favoring his left leg.

"Is that a police station?" Vic asks, seeing what look like cop cars or ambulances parked on their left.

"No idea. I need to rest," Dulce says.

"Me too," Vic seconds.

"Look, there's a bench. Let's go over there," she says, then stops in her tracks.

"I don't feel good. I'm going to be sick Vic."

"Can you make it to the beach restrooms?"

"No, it's getting ready to come up."

"Sand! Here's some sand!" Vic says helping Dulce over to the sand as she throws up.

Vic is rubbing Dulce's back as she is retching and then lets her up easy.

"Thank you, Vic. Let's go sit down. I feel faint."

They make it to the bench and plant themselves.

"I feel much better now," Dulce says.

Then, tilting her head back, she says, "It's so beautiful tonight. Smell that ocean breeze."

"Smells good. Look at that moon," Vic marvels. "It looks like there are two moons."

He puts his arm around her.

"If you're thinking about kissing me, don't," she cautions.

"I was thinking about it. I have vomit breath too. The moon is moving around in circles. I'm still drunk. The both of us are still drunk. Are we still drunk?"

"Sí, Vic, todavía estamos borrachos," Dulce says in Spanish. Then realizing she spoke Spanish, she says, "Sorry about that. I said, 'Yes, Vic, we're still drunk'. And we are."

"I can feel the swill in my veins. Can you teach me Spanish?"

"Absolutely," she replies. "We were loquacious today Vic."

"You like using big words with me, don't you honey?" he inquires.

"What big words sweetie?"

"Loquacious just now, metaphysical earlier today. Other big words."

"People often tell me I'm good with words. I was bilingual by the time I was six. Knowing English and Spanish facilitated my learning both languages. You're good with words too including big words. We're both good with words."

"I was doing my best to impress you today with my use of words," he says honestly.

They look at and listen to the ocean tides for a few minutes.

"You ready to leave?" Vic asks.

"Yes. This time you need to be on my right side so I can hold your left hand."

They get up from the bench and start making their way toward the hotel.

# Chapter 7

*Reasons*

After great effort Dulce and Vic manage to wobble over to the sidewalk along PCH.

"The hotel's right over there," Vic says. "My right thigh is on fire. It really does hurt. I hope I didn't break a bone. My back is on fire too. I need to get off my feet. My right hand is swollen."

"We'll make it, Vic. If you'd broken a bone you couldn't have danced in the gazebo and you couldn't limp now. All you need is rest."

They slowly approach the front door to the hotel. "Thank heaven we're here," Vic says as Dulce carefully opens the door for Vic and they go inside. The clerk who facilitated getting a room for Vic is still on duty. Vic instantly recognizes him.

"Good evening sir!" the clerk says cheerfully remembering Vic from earlier this afternoon and the favor he did for him for which he was generously rewarded.

"Good evening to you," Vic replies. "Don't call me sir I work for a living. You're still here?"

"I was just going off duty from the swing shift. Five minutes later and you would have missed me. I'm glad to see you again. Are you hurt?

I noticed you were limping when you came through the door and were being held up by this nice lady."

"I'm Vic and this is Dulce."

Not fully sure, Vic whispers a confirmation question to Dulce.

"You aren't Liesl, are you? I mean you are Dulce, correct?"

"Correct Vic," Dulce whispers back.

The clerk is ready to leave.

"My name is Charles. It was nice meeting you guys."

"Thanks for all your help today Charles," Vic says in sincere appreciation and gratitude.

"You are most welcome Vic. Have an enjoyable stay and have a good one."

Charles waves so long to Dulce and Vic as they stagger over to the elevator and step in.

"What's our room number?" she asks.

"Room number?" he replies, with a confused look on his face.

"Which room did you get so I know which floor button to push. You do have the key?"

"I have the key."

Vic reaches into his sport coat pocket and pulls out a tube of sunscreen and no key.

"I have the key," Vic says once more, tenderly taking his wallet out of his pants pocket with his swollen right hand. He checks every nook and cranny in his wallet. No key.

"I have the key," he says hoping third time is a charm. He reaches deep into both pants pockets. No key.

"Vic, you mean to tell me you lost the key?"

"Now I remember!" he says. "When you asked me to dance, I remember thinking to myself I don't want to lose the key because it was loose in my left pocket with my phone. You reached in my pants and pick pocketed me and stole my phone, remember that?

I am Sherlock Holmes and my detective skills are telling me when you withdrew my phone you also inadvertently mind you inadvertently withdrew my room key at the same time not meaning to and dropped it on the floor. It wasn't your fault Liesl. Our key is on the gazebo floor. Shall we go retrieve it?"

Dulce begins to laugh.

"No, Sherlock let's not walk up that long steep flight of stairs to retrieve it. You'll have to get a replacement key at the desk."

They walk out of the elevator and Dulce guides Vic to the front desk clerk.

"Yes sir, how may I help you?" the front desk clerk asks, smelling strong alcohol on their breaths. These folks are plastered he notices.

"My name is Victor Fontaine and this afternoon a fine young man Charles bent the rules for me after I gave him a one hundred dollar bill and after he bounced somebody from a room in order that I could have a romantic evening in a room at your fine hotel with this fine young lady Dulce.

Dulce and I, or Liesl as she is known in some social circles, were dancing in the gazebo a little while ago auditioning for parts in 'The Sound of Music' when she reached into my pants and grabbed my room key and threw it on the ground."

Dulce is desperately trying to put her hand over Vic's mouth. He swats her hand away and continues blabbing.

"That is interesting sir. I will have to mention this to Charles. You say you lost your key Mr. Fontaine?"

"That's right I lost my key and I'm Vic Fontaine. You might remember seeing me on TV. I'm the drug dealer who beat the rap."

The front desk clerk checks the terminal.

"You used an AMEX card?"
"Yes, I did. I don't leave home without it."
"May I see it Mr. Fontaine?"
"Of course," Vic says reaching for his wallet and discovers his wallet is missing.
"My wallet is gone!" Vic cries out.
"Did you pick pocket my wallet baby doll?" he asks Dulce.
"But you just had it. I saw you check your wallet for the key in the elevator," she says.
Then it hits her. The elevator!
"It must be in the elevator," she cries out rushing over to the elevator and pushing the open button.
Thank heaven she thinks to herself there it is. Dulce retrieves the wallet from the elevator floor.
"Here it is," she says happily.
Dulce takes out Vic's AMEX card and gives it to the front desk clerk.

"Just a moment Mr. Fontaine," the clerk says. After doing some transactions the clerk hands a room key to Vic, who has it taken away from him by Dulce. The clerk returns Vic's AMEX card to Dulce seeing she is the more sober of the two. That's not saying much.

"You are in Room 323 Mr. Fontaine. Check-out is at 11:00 AM and a complimentary continental breakfast is available at 7:00 AM."

"Thank you!" Dulce says for the both of them.
Vic, feeling magnanimous, wants to be sure he gives credit where credit is due.
"What is your name sir?" Vic asks the clerk.
"Paul."

"Paul, you be sure to thank Charles for all the help he was to me this afternoon. I think Charles has potential and will be moving up the management ladder at this fine establishment in no time. I can always tell when people are going places. Be sure to tell Charles."

"Rest assured I will tell Charles," Paul says, adding, "You can count on it."

"You are a gentleman and a scholar," Vic says as Dulce drags him away.

The get into the elevator.

Vic begins to panic once again.
"The key is missing! The key is missing!"
Vic begins to panic some more.
"My wallet is missing too!"
Dulce erupts in laughter realizing they aren't moving because they didn't push the button. She presses the button for the third floor.
"Chill Sherlock I have the room key and your wallet," she says continuing to laugh.

They reach the third floor and exit.

"Let me see, Room 332," Dulce says looking at the key. They approach Room 332. She inserts the key. Nothing. She tries again. Nothing again. Finally, after several more attempts she sees they are at the wrong room.

"Oops, my mistake," she says. "I could have sworn we were at Room 323. This is Room 332."
They lurch down the row of rooms arriving at their true destination. Dulce carefully cross-checks and verifies they are indeed at Room 323.

Vic takes the room key from Dulce's hand.

"I'll open the door. This is a job for your boyfriend. For the record I am not a wimp and don't you ever take pity on me."

Vic inserts the key and when he retracts it a negative buzz emits. He tries again. Another false start. Vic keeps trying and trying and gets false start after false start.

Dulce takes pity on him.

"Vic, you have to use finesse and cache to insert the key in and take it out at just the right time. You are incapable of performing that function at this time. I will show you how it's done."

Dulce tries a few times herself to no avail. She is receiving the same negative buzz like Vic.

"It's either a conspiracy to keep us apart, or that Paul guy clerk downstairs gave us a bad key."

Without warning the door to the room next door opens slightly. A man is staring at them through the crack in his door. "Anything wrong?" he asks.

"No, everything is under control," Vic tells the man.
"Yes. We can't get in our room. Can you please help us?" Dulce cajoles.

Without answering the man steps outside, takes the room key from Dulce, and in one clean fell swoop opens Room 323 for them.

"Thank you!" Dulce says in gratitude.
"You are a gentleman and a scholar," Vic says as the man returns to his room.

"Here we are lover," Vic says as he stumbles forward almost falling down as Dulce is able to block his fall enough to prevent him from crashing to the floor.

She guides him to the King-sized bed and takes off his sports jacket and lays him down. Dulce finds the two Ibuprofen pills he had showed her earlier. She fills a glass of water and gives it to Vic along with one pill.

"Take this tablet Vic it will help with your pain," she says. "Swirl the water around in your mouth it'll help get rid of the vomit taste." Vic does as he is told.

"Did you bring the luggage in?" he asks.
"We don't have luggage."
"We don't?"
"No, we don't Vic. We only have what we are wearing and carrying."

Dulce takes the other Ibuprofen pill in anticipation of warding off the inevitable bad hangover that is in the forecast for tomorrow.

Vic starts to think about things.

"My meter is expired! I'm going to get a parking ticket!"

"You're rich Vic you don't have to worry about that so much. And just because your meter is expired that doesn't mean you will get a ticket. You might luck out. Your luck has been pretty good today."

"What about your car?" he inquires.
"I didn't bring my car. Joaquin drove me."

Vic sees a clock radio on the night stand next to the bed.

"I'm going to put on my favorite oldies station honey," he says rolling over a couple of times on the bed. He reaches out to the clock radio and is able to find his station despite his wasted condition.

Dulce is smiling at Vic as she fluffs her hair watching him fiddle with the clock radio in the mirror. It looks like they will be sleeping together tonight. Make that sleeping. They are in no condition to do anything else and they desperately need sleep.

"Turn the radio down low, sweetie," Dulce says to Vic as she approaches the bed.

Vic is already half asleep as the radio is playing softly enough not to disturb their neighbors.

Dulce calls the front desk and asks Paul for an eight o'clock wake up call. Vic is still in his street clothes except for his sports jacket. She takes off his shoes and takes off her shoes and dress and slides in next to him so he is on her right.

"Wanna get under the covers?" he asks.
"This is fine, Vic. I'm too tired for an undercover operation."
"Move close to me," she says.
"With pleasure honey," he replies.

"Is it me, or is the room spinning?" Vic mumbles almost asleep.
"It's not you. The room is spinning for me too. Put your arm around me Vic."

Vic is lying next to Dulce on her right and puts his arm around her as they are snuggling side by side. Dulce takes his swollen right hand and begins to massage it as she presses it against her right breast.

"Are we boos?" he asks.
"Go to sleep," she replies.
"I love you," he says, whispering in her ear.
"Go to sleep now," she says, smiling enigmatically like the Mona Lisa.

They rapidly fall asleep due to extreme emotional, mental and physical exhaustion and high alcohol consumption.

The last part of the song 'Reasons' by the band 'Earth, Wind and Fire' is softly playing from the oldies station on the clock radio.

> *I can't find the reasons*
> *That my love won't disappear*
> *Can't find the reasons*
> *Why I love you, baby, my dear*
> *Can't find the reasons*
> *Wanna love you all night*
> *Can't find the reasons*
> *Gotta squeeze ya, real tight*